Fury (
Book One

FC

TO BAT, TO BOWL, TO DO

Become a Fury Cricketer.
Help defeat the sinister conspiracy
threatening the game we know and love.
Join the team as they use their bravery, skill
and courage to save world cricket!

LEG SIDE

OFF SIDE

Deep Fine Leg
Fine Leg
Leg Gully
Third Slip
Second Slip
First Slip
Leg Slip
Wicketkeeper
Third Man
Gully
Silly Point
Square Short Leg
Square Leg
Short Leg
Deep Square Leg
Forward Short Leg
Silly Mid On
Short Mid Wicket
Mid Wicket
Point
Cover
Silly Mid Off
Deep Mid Wicket
Extra Cover
Mid On
Bowler
Mid Off
Long On
Long Off

Welcome to The World of Fury Cricket

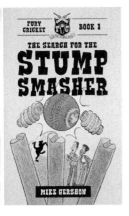

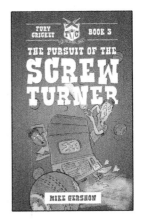

The Search For The Stump Smasher

By
Mike Gershon

Illustrations by Rory Walker

Dear Reader,

I've always loved cricket.

The excitement, the anticipation, the joy of seeing your team win.

Or of hitting the winning runs yourself.

I wanted to share that with you.

To give you not just a thrilling adventure story, but a gateway into the world of cricket.

A path.

A stepping stone.

Whether you play, watch or just dream about cricket, this book is for you.

And it's for all the thousands of cricketers who have been lighting up the stage for so long.

Maybe you'll be the next one.

Out there, in the middle of the pitch, sending down lightning-fast rockets.

Smashing sixes over midwicket.

Taking superhero catches.

Zipping mega-spinning leg breaks past the bat.

Or whipping off the bails with hands like whirlwinds.

Wherever you are, whatever your dream, get ready to join the Fury Cricket club, and help change the world of cricket forever!

Mike

For Catherine, Arthur and Thomas.

Chapter One:
An Umpire is Required

Eleven men, young and old, sat in eleven leather armchairs. There was one empty seat at the head of the table.

The walls of the room were covered in cricket bats, cricket jumpers, and pictures of famous cricketers. Except for one. That wall was stacked from floor to ceiling with dusty cricket books packed tightly onto dark wooden shelves.

One of the men drummed his fingers on the mahogany table. His fingernails were perfectly trimmed. As was his white moustache and what remained of his thin, grey hair.

'Damn nuisance having to wait on the little fellow. I never had to put up with these kinds of things when I was in charge.'

'And we never had the chance to achieve anything when you were in charge, Number Six. So be quiet and wait for Number One.'

Number Six, the old man with the neatly-trimmed moustache, tutted.

'Damn nuisance, that's what I say …'

But no one was listening to him.

They were all thinking about what was around the corner, and how they were going to take back control of the world of cricket.

'Your coat, sir?'

'Thank you, Meadows.'

'Will there be anything else, sir?'

'Yes, Meadows, there will be, as a matter of fact.'

'Follow me to the Larwood Suite; we'll need a drinks order taken.'

'Very good, sir.'

Frank Meadows, star batter in the Abbey Road Young Boys First XI, followed Number One down the hall.

Their feet pressed into the plush red carpet. It was soft and plump underfoot, cushioning their steps.

The two men rounded a corner and then ascended a wide flight of stairs.

They passed portraits of famous cricketers.

Bowlers, batters, wicketkeepers.

Cricketers who had done incredible things on the field of play.

Number One reached the Larwood Suite and pushed open the large, heavy door (complete with cricket-ball door handle) that led inside.

'Very good, Meadows, you have the drinks order. Now be a good chap and fetch those for us, will you?'

'Certainly, sir.' He half-bowed as he left. They liked that sort of thing here.

'Jolly good fellow, that', said Number Six as the door shut behind Frank Meadows.

'Deference. That's what's missing from cricket today'

'No recognition of the superior individual.'

'Not like it was when I was leading the Army XI on our tours of the colonies.'

Numbers One, Two, Three, Four, Five, Seven, Eight, Nine, Ten, Eleven and Twelve all looked at Number Six.

'Do shut up, Number Six', said Number One.

'There are no colonies anymore, and there haven't been for a very long time.'

Number Six started to speak, then thought better of it, and instead began inspecting his fingernails.

'Now, apologies for my lateness, gentlemen, but I had to attend to a minor matter on my way here. If we are all ready, we can get down to business.'

There was a general bobbing of heads and a rumble of agreement.

'Good. I have the documents.'

Number One pulled a brown leather briefcase onto his lap, flipped open the catches, and retrieved a thick wad of papers.

These were passed around the table, each man taking his own set of documents, until a much smaller pile returned to Number One.

'Everything is as we agreed?' asked Number Nine.

Number One nodded.

'Everything is as we agreed.'

'Any changes?' asked Number Eleven.

'No changes', said Number One.

'Fine. Then I suggest we move on and get the thing signed. All in favour?'

Number Eleven glanced up and down the table.

One by one, the rest of the group raised their hands.

'Then we are agreed', said Number Eleven. 'You've done your job well, Number One.'

Number One surveyed the room, looking at each of the men sat in front of him. This was his organization now. He ran it. He controlled it. He would take it where it needed to go. And no one would stand in his way. Not Number Six, not Number Eleven. Not anybody.

'Hang on there, ducky', said Number Six, leaning forward in his chair. 'I'm not signing anything without a witness.'

Number One raised an eyebrow.

'Very wise, Number Six. But you have eleven witnesses right here. Are they not good enough for you? Do you not trust them?'

The words hung in the air for a few moments.

'I don't trust a single one of them', bellowed Number Six, his moustache quivering. 'And I'm damn sure they don't trust me. I wouldn't trust me if I was them. Not one jot. What we need is an umpire. Someone independent.'

Frank Meadows took the small service elevator back up to the Larwood Suite. The twelve drinks rested on the green velvet surface of a drinks trolley.

The elevator dinged and the doors opened.

He pushed the caddy out onto the landing and made his way past a large landscape painting of a cricket ground in the Caribbean.

The artist had captured a quiet moment of play. The batters were halfway down the wicket, talking to each other between overs. The bowler was walking to the start of his run-up. Fielders were getting into position. A peaceful pause before the battle of bat and ball began again.

'Drinks, gentlemen', said Frank, as he entered the Larwood suite.

He couldn't help feeling as if he had interrupted an argument.

'The boy will do. He's the perfect fit. Independent. Unbiased.'

Number Six stood up and walked over to where Frank was standing.

'Serve the drinks, boy, there's a good chap. Then we have a little job for you. There's £100 in it if you swear to keep your mouth shut. What, what?'

Frank looked at Number One.

With a swift, dismissive gesture of his hand, Number One indicated to Frank that he should serve the drinks.

What did it matter, thought Number One, if this busboy-cum-waiter learned a little about their business?

What possible effect could it have on the success of his plan? And if it meant Number Six was satisfied, then so be it.

After Frank had served the drinks, a chair was brought across, and room was made in-between Number One and Number Twelve.

'Take a seat', said Number One, 'and remind me of your name.'

'Frank Meadows.'

'Good, good. Well, you see, Frank, my friends and I are engaged in a venture. An enterprise. We intend to work together for the good of cricket. To make it better, to be precise. And we are here today to finalise our agreement.

'I have prepared a contract for us all to sign. A contract that binds us together. And we need a witness.

'Do you know what a witness is, Frank?'

Frank shifted in his seat. He could feel twelve pairs of eyes upon him.

'Someone independent. Like an umpire. Who can confirm that everything took place, and that it was all legal, and that everyone was happy.'

Number One smiled.

It was a smile into which a person could fall, if they were not careful, and find themselves trapped.

It was a spider's web of a smile.

'There you are, Number Six. Frank is our umpire.'

'Do you need me to read the contract, sir? Only, I don't have much experience with that sort of thing. I'm more of a practical guy. Cricket's my main thing. Playing and coaching.'

Number One shook his head.

'No, no, no, Frank. You don't need to read all the boring legal mumbo-jumbo. It will simply be enough that you are a witness.

'Watch us sign the documents. Make sure we are all happy. Make sure we are signing them freely, and then you sign yourself.'

'Not bad for one hundred pounds, young chap, eh?' said Number Six, stroking his moustache.

'Sounds good to me', said Frank.

'Excellent: then we're agreed. Onwards we go. Onwards to the future.'

Number One raised his glass. Everyone else around the table did the same. Apart from Frank, who didn't have a glass. He raised his hand instead, out of politeness, and wondered whether he would use his £100 to buy a new cricket bat, or a set of shiny red match balls.

Chapter Two:
The Thirteenth Copy

Everyone was happy.

Number Six had his umpire. Number One had his signatures, and Frank had his £100. Twelve signed contracts sat in a neat pile at the end of the table.

'Another drink, gentlemen? To celebrate the start of our enterprise.'

A low, satisfied cheer came back.

'Frank, be so good as to get us another round of drinks.'

'Of course, sir: my pleasure.'

Frank gave a half-bow. Out of the corner of his eye, he could see the one they called Number Six smiling and nodding at this show of respect.

'One other thing, Frank.'

Number One reached out an arm and wrapped his thin, bony fingers around Frank's wrist.

He had a surprisingly strong grip, thought Frank, who winced a little as Number One pulled him back.

'Yes, sir?'

'Take these contracts and have them photocopied. Twelve copies of the top one will do. I want to keep the originals safe.'

'Of course, sir. I will do it as soon as I've brought the drinks.'

'No, I think you should do it first. Before the drinks.'

'Certainly, sir. Whatever you wish.'

'Priorities, Frank. Life is about priorities. And don't forget', he said, as he passed the pile of contracts across, 'you agreed to secrecy. So, you will speak of this to no one. Understood?'

Frank nodded.

'Good', said Number One, slapping the pile of papers now in Frank's hands.

'Off you go, then. We have much still to discuss in this room, and no need of an umpire to listen to what we say.'

Out in the corridor, Frank took a deep breath.

£100 was a lot of money.

What with rent, bills, food, and everything else, he rarely had much left over.

It was tough looking after yourself when you were only eighteen, and out in the world on your own.

As he pushed the drinks trolley back towards the lift, he paused in front of the painting.

How wonderful would it be, he thought, travelling the world, watching and playing cricket?

From the raging turners of the subcontinent to the hard, fast strips of Australia and the West Indies.

The seaming grass-tops of New Zealand, and the firm, bouncing pitches of South Africa.

It was a dream. And he knew he wasn't the only one who had it. Across the world, millions of people – children and adults – went to sleep dreaming of the same things. Some dreamt of batting, some dreamt of bowling. And even a few dreamt of wicket-keeping.

£100 wouldn't get him around the world. But it would get him some new kit he could use in his next match for the Abbey Road Young Boys First XI.

And he could still dream, couldn't he? After all, dreams don't cost a penny.

In the lift, he let his mind wander.[*]

He didn't mind working at The Ancient Assembly of Cricket.

He rather liked it.

Yes, some of the people you came across were rather strange. Like that lot in the Larwood Suite. They all seemed to call each other Number something-or-other.

Which was odd when you came to think about it.

They must have names, he thought. Real names. Not just numbers.

Everyone has a name. Some people even have two or three or four. Ian Botham, for example, was also called Beefy. Rahul Dravid was called The Wall. And Mike Hussey was called Mr Cricket.

It all seemed a bit odd. Calling each other Number One, Number Six, and so on.

What were they trying to hide?

Why all the secrecy?

---

[*] A wandering mind is not good for a fielder. If left to its own devices, the mind can wander so very far from the field of play that it is a great surprise when the ball suddenly drops in front of you, from out of the sky. And even more of a shock when your teammates start yelling at you for missing a catch you never even knew about in the first place.

And what exactly was this enterprise that Number One had been talking about?

He had said it was something that would make cricket better. That didn't sound like the kind of thing that needed to be kept secret. In fact, it sounded like the kind of thing people would want to hear about.

In the photocopying room, Frank had a quiet discussion with himself.

Had he been sworn to secrecy?

Yes.

Did that mean he couldn't look at the contract, to see what it was all about?

Well, strictly speaking, no.

As long as he didn't tell anyone what he discovered, he would be OK. That way, he wouldn't be breaking any promises.

And Number One had never said he couldn't read the contract. What he actually said was that he didn't *need* to read it.

Anyway, if he was going to photocopy it, he'd have to take a look. Otherwise, how would he know that he was photocopying the right pages? The worst thing would be if he made a mistake.

Number One would not want him to make a mistake. He seemed like the kind of person who reacted badly to mistakes.

Number One would want the photocopying to be accurate.

He would want everything to be correct.

So really, when you thought about it, Frank had no choice. He would have to look at the contract. Not to satisfy his curiosity, you understand. But to make sure that he did the photocopying right. Without any mistakes.

And he would just have to remember not to tell anyone what was written inside.

Frank rubbed his chin.

He was pleased with himself.

That bit of thinking had been like playing a tricky delivery from a mystery spinner. If you concentrated and watched what you were doing, you had a decent chance of coming out OK.

He shut the door of the photocopying room and slid the drinks trolley in front of it in case anybody tried to enter while he was reading.

He picked up two copies of the contract.

With the first, he carefully removed the staple, separated the pages, and put the loose sheets into the photocopier. He pressed a few buttons and set up the machine to print twelve copies, stapled, in black and white.

It would take a good few minutes. Which was perfect. The right amount of time to sit down and see what this business was all about.

With a mechanical sigh of relief, the photocopier completed its job and powered down.

The noise of the machine faded, and the room was silent, except for the hum of the fluorescent ceiling lights and Frank's soft breathing.

He flipped the pages of the contract over, looked again at the first page, and sank down into a brown plastic chair next to the wall.

He had been pacing around the room for the last five minutes.

It was extraordinary.

How could he keep it a secret?

He'd never heard anything like it in his life.

There was no way he could keep this to himself. It was too big.

Too shocking.

Too much to ignore.

He stood up, in a trance. He felt himself walking over to the photocopier. It was as if someone else was controlling his movements. He watched as he took the loose sheets of the first contract, slipped them back into the copy tray and then pressed the big green button on the small display screen.

He waited as the machine did its work.

He listened as the staple crunched into the top right-hand corner of the thirteenth copy.

He reached over and took the copy from the top of the pile. Then he folded it up and slipped it into his inside jacket pocket.

It was a moment that would change his life forever. And one that would change the course of cricket the world over.

Chapter Three:
The League of
The Stuffed Shirts

rank returned to the Larwood Suite, his heart beating faster after what he had discovered, his mind worrying that he would be caught by Number One. That the man would wrap his strong bony fingers around Frank's wrist, reach inside his jacket pocket and extract the stolen photocopy.

His fear was misplaced.

On entering the suite, Number One scarcely looked at him. The room was thick with a blue-grey haze and the bitter smell of cigar smoke. Solemn conversations were happening between different members of the group.

Over his shoulder, Number One told Frank to leave the caddy, with the drinks and the contracts, by the door. He then dismissed him and told him there would be another £100 for him at reception at the end of the day, to thank him for his attentive service.

Frank started to bow on his way out, then remembered the contract and immediately straightened up.

He couldn't risk one of them seeing it poking out as he leaned forward.

'Typical', harrumphed Number Six.'

'Lad's got his money so he stops showing respect. Wouldn't have happened when I was in charge …'

The rest of the day passed, as slow as a long hot day in the field.

Frank had a range of duties to complete. Polishing trophies, dusting portraits, setting tables for dinner. The usual routine.

Today he also had to sweep the area at the front of the building, through which dignitaries from the world of cricket would be arriving that evening for a gala dinner.

As he swept, he wondered what it would be like to be a dignitary. To have people sending you invitations to lavish meals and important events.

The rest of the time, his mind raced and whizzed and whirred, thinking about the contract and its contents.

He was desperate to get home. Desperate to unlock the door to his small, cramped bedsit. Desperate to draw all the curtains and sit down on the sofa that doubled up as his bed, and look again at what he had read that morning.

After what felt like one of the longest days of his life, the clock struck five and he was free to leave.

Most days, on finishing work he would head to the changing rooms, put on his cricket gear, and spend a few hours honing his batting technique in the nets.

That was the best thing about working at The Ancient Assembly of Cricket. You had free use of the indoor and outdoor nets when you weren't working. And that included the bowling machine.*

He could spend hours batting, whether it was against real live humans, or the finely balanced repetition of the machine.

Sometimes, he would fill a whole evening practicing one type of shot against one type of delivery.

Forward defensives against in-swing. Sweeps against off-spin. Square cuts against short-pitched fast bowling.

---

* Not to be confused with a bawling machine, which was designed by an ingenious student who wanted to measure how loudly his headmaster shouted when trying to make himself heard in the school canteen.

The more he practiced, the better he got. It didn't always happen overnight. Sometimes it would take weeks to get better at a particular shot, or against a certain type of bowler.

But he was persistent. He was dogged.

He didn't give up.

Tonight would be different, though.

No practice.

No batting.

He had something more important to do.

Frank lived at the top of a mansion block. At one time in the distant past, the whole floor had belonged to a single family. Now, it was carved up into sixteen bedsits, each one a little smaller than the last.

Frank's bedsit was number sixteen, the smallest of the lot.

The cramped room contained a sofa-bed, a miniature cooker, a sink, three cupboards, a television, a bookcase full of cricket books, and a corner piled high with cricket kit.

Next to the cooker was a thin door leading to a tiny bathroom big enough to fit one person, as long as they didn't breathe out too much.

Frank undid his tie, loosened his top button, and slung his cricket bag onto the floor.

He was still wearing the smart navy uniform he wore while he worked.

He flopped down on the sofa and reached inside his jacket.

For a moment, he panicked.

The contract wasn't there!

He leaped from the sofa and was about to race out of the door to retrace his steps when he realized he had felt for the contract on the wrong side.

He relaxed, sat back down again, and dug a hand into his other inside pocket, where he found the contract, just as he had left it.

There was an old wooden table in front of his sofa, where he put his feet when he was watching television. Or where he left his cricket magazines before he went to bed.

With a quick sweep of his arm, he pushed the half-read *Cricketers* and *Wisden Cricket Monthlies* onto the floor.

Then he unfolded the contract, taking great care as he smoothed out the creases, and placed it on the table.

Leaning forwards, he began to read for the second time the incendiary document that had been signed by the twelve visitors to the Larwood Suite.

It began thus:

'We, The League of the Stuffed Shirts, do hereby agree to work in unison to return cricket to its rightful order. Together, we will use all our resources to ensure that only those we deem of the right type will be able to play professional cricket. We will bring about a new cricketing landscape. Playing will be for the few. Watching will be for the many.'

As Frank read, the words swirled through his mind, demanding to be heard. He understood them — but also, he didn't. Some of the things he was reading seemed too crazy to be true.

The contract continued:

'We consider ourselves the custodians of cricket. The protectors of the game. We will turn back the tide of progress, and in its place there will be order. Those who are worthy will be restored to their rightful place. The rich, the powerful, the wealthy. The well-connected, the well-educated. Those with the right names and the right backgrounds. These will be the players of the game. These will be the ones allowed to craft cricket's future. For the rest, there will be the chance to watch. And for them, that will be enough.'

Page after page he read. Each one more shocking than the last. And then he came to the final page. The one with the signatures.

He shook his head.

It was the same as when he had read it in the photocopier room. Somehow, he had thought it might be different.

But no.

There were no names. No real names. Instead, there were the names he had heard in the Larwood Suite:

Number One
Number Two
Number Three
Number Four
Number Five
Number Six
Number Seven
Number Eight
Number Nine
Number Ten
Number Eleven
Number Twelve

And next to each one there was a signature. But these were scrawls. They were impossible to read. Impossible to pick apart. They provided no clue as to who their authors were.

He picked up his copy of the contract and held it close to his face.

He squinted and tilted his head, trying to decipher the names hidden inside the messy scribbles.

It was hopeless.

He tossed the contract onto the table, slumped back onto the sofa, and sighed.

On the floor below, D.K. Chatterjee, one-time opening bowler and swashbuckling batter for the Bidhannagar Sporting club, West Bengal, was tying his black bow-tie, ready for the evening ahead.

The entire floor was his home, because D.K. Chatterjee was a wealthy man.

In his youth (which was many years in the past) he had dreamed of becoming a professional cricketer. It had been his eternal hope that one day he might even play for India, opening the bowling in a home test match.

However, many obstacles had stood in his way.

First, there had been the poverty he and his family had faced.

Second, there was the difficulty of balancing his cricket with the need to earn money to support his younger brothers and sisters.

Third, there was the fact that for some of his coaches, his face didn't fit. And they had made it harder for him to progress than it was for others.

But D.K. Chatterjee had been born with an aptitude for action.

He was not one who would let obstacles stand in his way. If he couldn't climb over something, he would find a way around it. If he couldn't find a way around, he would dig a tunnel and pop up on the other side.

And that was what he had done.

At the age of fourteen, he had started making his own cricket bats and selling these to friends and family.

At the age of twenty-two, he set up his first factory, manufacturing cricket bats for sale through the whole of West Bengal.

At the age of thirty-five, his cricket bats were being bought by budding cricketers across the entirety of India.

D.K. Chatterjee bats were famed for their quality and value for money.

And by the time he was fifty, his bats were sold on every continent on earth.

From Kingston to Pretoria, Galle to Wellington, and everywhere in between, D.K. Chatterjee bats were loved by cricketers of all ages and backgrounds.

Today, D.K. was approaching his dotage. He no longer took an active role in the design, manufacture, and sale of bats. He left that to his sons and daughters.

He was retired.

And he had bought this flat so he could be close to The Ancient Assembly of Cricket, whenever he was in London.

Which was usually for about six months a year.

He had other homes around the world. And each one was near a cricket ground. Wherever he went, he took the opportunity to see as much cricket as he could.

And he was as happy watching a bunch of amateurs knock up on a patch of unused grass as he was watching the greatest players of the age go head-to-head in the cauldron of test cricket, or the furnace of T20.

His wife, Suravi, had long ago given up trying to pull D.K. away from his love of cricket. She contented herself with the knowledge that cricket provided her husband with great joy. And over the years, she had come to enjoy it as well.

At the moment, Suravi was in India, with the Chatterjees' youngest daughter, who had recently given birth to her second child. Having grandmother on hand to help was much appreciated by all.

This created a problem for D.K.

Despite his great success in life, despite all he had done to pull himself up from his lowly roots and establish himself the world over, he had never mastered the art of tying a bow-tie.

Every time he tried, the fabric ended up hanging from his collar like wilted flowers sagging over the edge of a vase.

Normally he would ask Suravi to tie it for him; or he would wear a pre-tied bow-tie with a clip.

An hour of searching the vast apartment had been unsuccessful on that front.

There were no pre-tied bow-ties to be found.

As he looked at himself in the mirror, smartly dressed in a black tuxedo and white shirt, silvery moustache trailing past the edge of his lips, an idea came to him.

Upstairs, there lived a young man called Frank Meadows.

D.K. had seen him many times, practicing his batting in the nets, and playing exquisite cover-drives for the Abbey Road Young Boys First XI.*

They had chatted on more than one occasion. And they had got on rather well, sharing a similar passion for all things cricket.

A few minutes later, having twice knocked on the wrong door, D.K. found his man.

---

* An exquisite cover-drive is a beautiful thing. It is like watching a rainbow emerge from the head of a sunflower, or like seeing a firework explode into a drumbeat of colour. Many batters over the years have mastered the cover-drive. David Gower was famed for his elegant drives, described as being like graceful, liquid movements of the bat. After cricket, he became a highly successful commentator as well.

Chapter Four:
A Partnership Begins

rank jumped out of his seat when he heard the knocking.

Could it be them? Were The League of the Stuffed Shirts outside his bedsit, ready to take back the contract he stole and do who knows what to him in the process?

His throat felt dry. His shoulders tensed.

The knocking returned.

He snatched up the contract and looked for somewhere to hide it.

'Mr Meadows?'

The voice filtered through the door.

'Are you there, Mr Meadows?'

It was a familiar voice, but Frank couldn't put his finger on who it belonged to.

'I was hoping you could lend me a hand, Mr Meadows, if it isn't too much trouble?'

Frank scanned the bedsit. His mind was buzzing. He couldn't think straight.

'One minute', he shouted. 'Give me a minute.'

He looked one way, then the other.

The bedsit was so small that there were few, if any, hiding places.

Then he saw the sofa.

'Ah, Mr Meadows, thank you so much for answering.'

Frank stood in the doorway of his bedsit. His hair was ruffled. A single bead of sweat escaped from somewhere above his ear and trickled down the side of his face.

He raised a hand and tried to wipe it away. It took three attempts before he succeeded.

'Mr Chatterjee, what a pleasant surprise. How are you?'

'D.K. — call me D.K., please.'

Frank guessed that Mr Chatterjee was attending the gala dinner that evening, at The Ancient Assembly of Cricket.

It was an annual event arranged by the Organisation for International and National Cricket. OINC for short.[*]

Tonight, the great and the good of the cricketing world would come together to discuss the game and to elect new representatives to the OINC governing body.

---

[*] No pigs were harmed in the making of this acronym.

Frank knew for definite that Mr Chatterjee was one of the great and the good. Though he didn't behave as you'd expect a cricketing big-wig to behave.

He was always polite and friendly, easy to talk to, and full of questions about how you were, and what was happening with your game.

'Are you going to the event tonight, Mr Chatterjee?' asked Frank, pointing at the tuxedo.

'Please, please, Mr Meadows — D.K. You must call me D.K. Only my bank manager calls me Mr Chatterjee. And that's when he wants a loan.'

They both laughed.

D.K. asked if he could come in for a minute as he needed Frank's help with a small problem he couldn't manage on his own.

Frank stepped back and let Mr Chatterjee into his room.

He felt embarrassed by the bedsit's small size.

'This is cosy', said D.K. 'And I see you have a good bookshelf.' He pointed at the cricket books next to the window. 'Always important, that, Mr Meadows. A good bookshelf is a sound investment.'

'When you have a good book to read, the world becomes both bigger and brighter, don't you think?'

He smiled and pointed to his bow-tie.

'My little problem, Mr Meadows. Do you know how to tie a bow-tie?'

As luck would have it, Frank Meadows did know how to tie a bow-tie. Growing up, his mother had been keen for her son to look as smart as possible when attending family gatherings.

Much to his annoyance, he had been made to wear a bow-tie on many of those occasions.

Even more annoying was the fact that he came from a large family. Which meant there were lots of family gatherings throughout the year.

By the time he was nine, he could tie a bow-tie one-handed, with his eyes shut.[*]

Frank invited Mr Chatterjee to sit down on the sofa. After all, it was the only place a visitor could sit.

Meanwhile, Frank perched on the small table.

Mr Chatterjee tilted his head back, flicked up his collar, and let Frank go to work.

The process was quick and painless.

---

[*] Not something to be recommended for beginner bow-tiers. Better to start with two hands, a pair of open eyes, a magnifying glass, a mirror, an instructional video and a back-up clip-on bow-tie, just in case.

The total opposite of having to bowl with an old ball to Viv Richards in the middle of a test match you were well on your way to losing.

'There we go, Mr Chatterjee. All done.'

'D.K., please — no need for the formality, Mr Meadows.'

Frank laughed.

'OK, he said, have it your way. All done, D.K.'

'Thank you, Frank: you have been a great help. If there is anything I can do for you, you must let me know.'

D.K. turned down his collar, felt the expertly tied bow-tie, and smiled.

'An excellent job', he said.

Frank wavered.

There was a moment of silence.

It was a slightly uncomfortable silence.

He knew D.K. Chatterjee was not a member of The League of the Stuffed Shirts. Or, at least, that he had not been in the Larwood Suite.

'What is it, Frank?' asked D.K. 'Do you need a job, maybe? Don't be embarrassed to ask. We all want to get on in the world.'

Frank hesitated.

'No … it's not that …'

He didn't know whether he could trust D.K. He felt like he could. He seemed like an honourable man.

Was that enough, though? Wasn't he taking a huge risk if he told him what he knew?

But who else could he tell about what he'd read?

He closed his eyes.

'There's something I'd like you to look at for me, if you don't mind.'

D.K. Chatterjee raised his eyebrows.

'Is it something you've written?'

Frank shook his head.

'No ... it's something ... I've stolen.'

The atmosphere in the room changed. Mr Chatterjee shifted in his seat then looked Frank straight in the eyes.

'You've stolen something, Frank? Really? You must know that it's wrong to steal. Whatever made you do that?'

'You shouldn't be asking me to read it, Frank. You should be taking it back to whomever it belongs to, and apologizing for your error.'

'You don't understand, Mr Chatterjee. It's ... I didn't ... I'm not a thief.'

'Honestly. Please, just read it. I won't tell anyone.'

D.K. Chatterjee was on the verge of getting up and walking out of the bedsit. He wondered if he had misjudged the character of Frank Meadows.

But there was something in Frank's voice that told him maybe not.

So, he remained on the sofa and asked Frank to explain himself.

'There was this meeting … they were all calling each other Number this and Number that … I was working, fetching drinks … there was a contract they were signing … they asked me to be a witness … they gave me £100 then left another £100 for me at reception … I had to photocopy it for them … and I decided to read it …'

D.K. Chatterjee slowly nodded his head.

'I see', he said. 'Curiosity has almost killed the cat in this situation. You are not the first person to suffer this fate, Frank. But the best thing to do is to make amends. You must return what you've taken, apologise, and face the consequences.'

Frank ran his fingers along the edge of the table.

He was starting to regret telling Mr Chatterjee about what he'd done.

But there weren't a lot of options left.

He reached forward and slid his hand under one of the sofa cushions.

Surprised, Mr Chatterjee swayed to one side and watched Frank pull a crumpled photocopy from beneath the light-green cushion.

'Read it, please', said Frank, pushing the contract towards D.K. 'You must read it.'

Twenty minutes later, D.K. Chatterjee stood up.

Frank had watched, in silence, as he had read the contract for a first, second, and then a third time.

He continued watching as D.K. inspected the signatures, even going so far as to bring the copy of the contract right up in front of his face.

Eventually, he spoke.

'You are an honourable man, Frank Meadows. And you made a brave choice sharing this with me.'

'It was the right choice.'

Frank felt every muscle in his body relax as relief swept through him. It was like a wave of sunlight washing into a room when the curtains are drawn back.

'I recognize some of these signatures', said D.K., jabbing his finger at the page. 'And I am appalled at what they are trying to do.'

Frank gasped.

'You know who they are? You know who Number One is?'

D.K. nodded.

'I recognise two of the signatures. Recognise them very well.'

'How?' asked Frank.

'Because', said D.K., leaning forwards, brandishing the contract in his right hand, 'they have personally signed contracts with my company for the supply of cricket bats.'

Chapter Five:
The Conspiracy
Reveals Itself

he leader – the person who calls himself Number One – is Jago Lilywhite Grace.'

'What about Number Six, do you know him?'

'I do. Not the nicest chap, I'm afraid to say. His name is Sir Muirhead Gassington.'

D.K. Chatterjee stood up.

'This document is very serious, Frank. Very serious indeed. Grace and Gassington may not be well-liked, but they are rich, powerful, and well-connected. I daresay the rest of the people on this list are too.

'When you read it, did you understand it?'

Frank shrugged his shoulders.

'Kind of … yes, I think so …'

'Let me summarise it for you.'

'The League of the Stuffed Shirts is a group of wealthy, powerful men.'

'That is who was meeting in the Larwood Suite today. They do not like the fact that cricket can be played by anybody – man, woman, boy, girl, rich, or poor. They believe that access to cricket should be restricted. They believe that only certain types of people should be allowed to play cricket.'

'In this document they make an agreement. They agree that between the twelve of them they will work together, in secret, to bring about a fundamental change in cricket across the world.'

'It says they will work tirelessly to ensure that cricket can only be played by the rich and powerful.'

'They want to prevent everybody else from playing. Everybody. Man, woman, boy, girl. Their aim is to ensure the playing of cricket is fenced off. Available only to a select few.'

'They want to limit the rest of the world to watching cricket. Nothing more.'

'And do you know what else, Frank? They have already started on their mission! This document is not the beginning of their attempts. It is the end of the first stage.'

'It states that all twelve members of The League of the Stuffed Shirts have been working their way towards positions of cricketing power in their respective countries.'

'This, Frank, is a conspiracy. A global power-grab. It is not confined to England. No, no. This group are attempting to gain control of cricket across the entire world.'

'And the reason they met today, Frank. The reason they were in the Larwood Suite. The reason you stumbled across this, this ... plot, is because they have already done most of their work.'

'Tonight, at the OINC gala, hundreds of cricketing power-brokers from around the world will be voting on who should take seats on the OINC board.'

'Including who will take the seat of Governor.'

'That person is the leader of OINC. And, as a result, the leader of the cricketing universe.'

'And guess who is favourite to be elected?'

Frank opened his mouth and quietly breathed the name:

'Number One. Jago Lilywhite Grace.'

'Correct', said D.K. 'And chances are that Sir Muirhead and a fair few of the others on this list are standing for election as well.'

'By the end of the night, they'll have total control over cricket across the world. And we'll be powerless to stop them.'

D.K. Chatterjee walked over to the window and drew back the curtains.

From here, there was an almost perfect view of The Ancient Assembly of Cricket. It was the thing Frank liked most about the place.

The old man looked at the ornate, decorated buildings and the neatly-cut crisp green grass of the pitches.

He watched as young boys and girls, men and women, practiced their batting, their bowling, and their fielding.

'We have to do something', said Frank. 'We can't let this happen. Cricket is for everybody. Nobody should be told they can't play, whoever they are.'

'Wise words, Frank. Wise words from a young mind.'

D.K. Chatterjee turned away from the window.

'Have you ever been to a gala dinner, Frank? And do you own a tuxedo?'

The answer to both questions was 'no'.

Frank Meadows found himself back inside The Ancient Assembly of Cricket. Only, this time, he looked like a hungry penguin.

He was wearing one of D.K. Chatterjee's old tuxedos, and sitting at a circular table in a cavernous, brightly-decorated ballroom, along with one thousand other guests, and a small army of waiters and waitresses, all trained in the arts of silver service.[*]

---

[*] Silver service is an extremely fancy way of food being served to diners at important meals. If you can convince your parents to train in the art of silver service, you can enjoy the experience at home, although no child has yet managed to achieve this. It should also be noted that the art of gold service

D.K. had whisked Frank downstairs to his apartment. After rifling through the biggest wardrobe Frank had ever seen, he'd produced a tuxedo that looked like it hadn't been worn in at least a decade.

It fitted Frank. Not well. But it fitted.

It reminded him of being young and having to wear his cousins' cast-off clothes, and of his mum telling him that he would grow into them. Completely ignoring the fact that he would have to get by, looking like a deflated balloon, until her prophecy was fulfilled.

D.K. had a spare ticket, due to his wife's absence. As she was in India, it meant Frank could join his new ally at the gala dinner.

Eight others sat with them at their table. Frank didn't recognize anyone. But they all knew Mr Chatterjee.

In fact, Mr Chatterjee seemed to know a great many people. Or a great many people seemed to know him, because he did have to ask some of those who came over for a chat what their names were, and how they were acquainted.

Before they arrived, D.K. had explained the plan. It was simple, he claimed. But Frank wasn't so sure.

---

remains a mystery. If you find out what it involves, send me a note and some pictures.

It went something like this.

Frank would come to the gala dinner as D.K.'s guest. When the meal was in full swing, they would both make their excuses and exit the ballroom.

Frank would show D.K. to the Larwood Suite, using his security pass to unlock any doors barring their way.

Once inside, the two of them would search for evidence that could go alongside the stolen copy of the contract.

What they really needed was something identifying the members of The League of the Stuffed Shirts.

That way, they could present the assembled group of cricketing movers and shakers with enough evidence to immediately put an end to the plot, preventing the election of Jago and his cronies to the OINC board.

In the ballroom, thinking about the plan, Frank felt nervous.

As Mr Chatterjee talked and smiled and gestured to the stream of people who came to greet him, Frank looked around the room, trying to spot Jago, Sir Muirhead, or any of the ten other people who had been in the Larwood Suite.

He didn't know whether he wanted to see them or not.

If he did, they might recognize him and ask what, precisely, a lowly employee like him was doing at such an important event.

On the other hand, if he didn't see them, that might mean they had already spotted him and were keeping their distance.

His head was in a spin.

How could anyone hatch such a dastardly plan as the one The League of the Stuffed Shirts had come up with?

He could not understand why people would want to restrict the playing of cricket.

To him, it was a fantastic game. One that he loved. And one that millions across the world loved as well, in countries near and far.

Surely, the best thing was for more people to play cricket? And for everybody to feel like they could play — whoever they were, and wherever they came from?

He shook his head.

Sometimes he struggled to understand the world of adults.

A world he had entered only six months ago, after his eighteenth birthday celebrations.

This Jago character had strange motives.

As did the other members of the League.

Maybe he would understand it better as he grew older.

But he doubted it.

Mr Chatterjee was old, wasn't he? And he felt the same way as Frank did. So, it wasn't about age. There was something else.

He sighed.

It had all been a lot to take in.

A big, red-faced man in a scarlet-coloured jacket walked onto the stage and started ringing a brass bell.

'Ladies and Gentlemen', he bellowed. 'May I have your attention, please.'

His voice was a foghorn. It blared across the ballroom, loud enough to quieten the conversations people were having at their dining tables.

'The first course will be served promptly. If you have not done so already, please return to your places.'

Frank watched as men and women from the four corners of the cricketing world flowed between tables in search of their seats.

The smell of hot, spicy soup and freshly baked bread wafted into the ballroom.

It had been a while since Frank had eaten. The excitement — and the stress — of the last few hours had made him hungry.

47

He took a crisp white napkin from the table and unfolded it.

A cricket ball was embroidered in the top left corner, above a bat and a pair of wicket-keeping gloves.

As he was about to lay the napkin across his lap, ready to eat, he felt a firm tap on his shoulder.

His heart sank.

Couldn't Mr Chatterjee wait to begin their search for evidence until after the starter?

He turned in his chair, ready to protest.

And looked straight into the small, angry eyes of Sir Muirhead Gassington.

Chapter Six:
Dinner is Served

mposter!' hissed Sir Muirhead, jabbing a fat, quivering finger into Frank's face.

'Imposter!' he repeated, the jowls of his neck shaking with rage.

'Sir Muirhead ... I ...'

Frank's attempt at explaining his presence was cut off.

'How dare you sneak in here, you bounder! There is a strict policy in place. Invitation only. And invitations are given solely to those worthy of attending such a prestigious event.'

'Which does not include drinks-ferrying, door-opening, riff-raff commoners like you!'

Sir Muirhead's face had turned the colour of beetroot.

'I'll have to deal with you myself. Can't rely on security for anything these days. Come here!'

The knight of the realm bent forwards and grabbed the lapels of Frank's jacket.

Frank could smell the rotten stink of Sir Muirhead's breath creeping up his nostrils.

'Come here, you wretch! I'll kick your backside half-way down the Edgware Road.'

Frank clamped his hands onto Sir Muirhead's forearms and tried to wrestle him away.

Every time he tried to speak, Sir Muirhead drowned him out.

The commotion was drawing the attention of people sitting nearby.

'Absolute disgrace! How dare you sneak your way in here …'

Sir Muirhead struggled against Frank's youthful strength. The older man, however, had bulk on his side.

He was about to drop his shoulder in an effort to wrench Frank out of his seat when a calm, quiet voice spoke from somewhere behind his right ear.

'I really wouldn't do that, Gassington, old boy. You'll get yourself thrown out.'

'What's that?' barked Sir Muirhead, looking over his shoulder in the direction of the voice.

D.K. Chatterjee continued speaking, in a tone quite different from the one he had used when talking to Frank.

This was the cut-glass burr of ancient London clubs.

Smoke-filled rooms lined with leather-bound books.

And deep armchairs stuffed with snoozing pensioners in tweed trousers.

'My guest will be most upset if I have to ask the security guards to escort you from the premises.'

'Your guest?!' spluttered Sir Muirhead.

'This boy is a door-opener. A picture-polisher. He's nothing better than a drinks-fetcher!'

'And what a fine drinks-fetcher he is', said D.K. 'not to mention an outstanding prospect as a middle-order batter.'

D.K. slipped into the chair next to Frank and reached for his napkin.

He shot a dismissive glance towards Sir Muirhead.

'Are you still here, Gassington? Do you need me to send you a telegram explaining that Mr Meadows is my guest?'*

The embattled knight relaxed his grip.

Frank felt himself sink back into the padded chair.

Sir Muirhead Gassington narrowed his eyes and snorted. It was the kind of snort that could suck a tablecloth up someone's nose, past their brain and out through their ears, if they weren't careful.

---

* Telegrams are what the internet was like before computers were invented.

'How did you know my name, boy?'

The question was laced with suspicion.

Sir Muirhead ran his tongue across the front of his teeth. An animal preparing to pounce on its prey.

Frank gripped the side of his chair.

He realised his mistake.

He had used Sir Muirhead's name.

But that morning, in the Larwood Suite, he had only heard him referred to as Number Six.

'My dear Muirhead', said D.K. 'What do you take me for? Do you think I am a barbarian? Of course Mr Meadows knows your name. I have spent the last half-hour explaining to him who all the most important people in attendance are.'

'He is only a young man. How could he know that you are Sir Muirhead, that over there is P.U.D. Smith, that sitting three tables down from us is Rene De Klerk, and that beside the stage, resplendent in a light-blue jacket, is Ravichandran Talwar?'

'Mr Meadows has been getting an education, Muirhead. And you are but a small part of that. Important, yes. But also, small.'

'You do believe in the importance of education, don't you, Gassington?'

Sir Muirhead flexed his jaw and began to speak, but decided against it.

His nostrils flared and his moustache quivered, along with his reddened jowls.

He looked at Frank, turned to D.K., and then, without a word, fastened the brass button of his royal-blue blazer and stalked away, in the direction of his own table.

Frank let out a low whistle of relief.

D.K. watched Sir Muirhead disappear into the throng of guests.

He turned to the other eight diners at their table.

'You can always rely on Gassy for entertainment, can't you?'

He laughed and clapped his hands together.

The rest of the table shared the joke and then returned, smiling, to their previous conversations.

It was as if D.K. was the director and they were his cast.

'That was a close one', whispered Frank.

'Too close', said D.K.

'I'm sorry I used his name', said Frank. 'It just came out.'

'Don't worry about it', said D.K. 'that was very instructive.'

The two of them were speaking in low, hushed voices as the hot soup and freshly baked bread started to arrive.

'What do you mean?' asked Frank.

'They're on edge', said D.K. 'Sir Muirhead lost his cool. He almost caused an embarrassment. If I was in Number One's shoes, the last thing I would be looking for is unwanted attention.'

'Do you think they know?' asked Frank. He could feel a few drops of sweat pricking out across the back of his neck.

'I think Muirhead is suspicious', said D.K. 'and that isn't good for us. We may need to bring our timings forward.'

As they finished speaking, two waiters reached over and placed bowls of hot soup in front of them, followed by side-plates with bread-rolls and butter. So fresh were the rolls that steam from the oven was still whisping upwards from their crusts.

Frank looked hungrily at the food.

And then, in a whirl of movement, D.K. knocked his own bowl of soup onto the floor.

It landed between the two of them, making a dull thumping noise as it hit the carpet. Thick orange liquid flew out, splashing into the air and spattering Frank's trouser leg.

Flecks of soup found their way onto D.K.'s shiny black shoes.

Immediately, two waiters were upon them, fussing and apologising.

Accepting unquestioning blame for the unfortunate incident.

Urging forgiveness for their error.

D.K. stood up and inspected his shoes.

He patted one of the waiters on the arm and explained that it was entirely his own fault.

A gush of further apologies sprang from the mouths of all involved.

The first waiter apologised for what had happened.

D.K. apologised for being so clumsy.

The second waiter apologised for the shape of the bowls and the liquidity of the soup.

Frank stood up and apologised for being in the way of the clean-up operation.

D.K. apologised to the table for all the fuss.

The two waiters apologised in unison, deeply saddened that the unfortunate incident had forced D.K. to issue an apology to the other diners.

Frank apologised to the waiters, but he didn't really know what for. It just seemed like the right thing to do.

'Sorry.'

'Sorry.'

'Sorry.'

'So terribly sorry.'

'Not at all, I'm the one who should be sorry.'

'Please, if anyone is to be sorry it should be me.'

'Sorry.'

'Frank, perhaps we should vacate the area so these two gentlemen can clear up the mess I have made? We must find a bathroom we can use to wash some of this soup off before it stains, don't you think?'

Frank nodded his agreement.

'Yes, absolutely. So sorry, once again.'

D.K. ushered Frank away from the table, and in the direction of a large pair of teak swing-doors that led from the ballroom into a brightly-lit foyer.

Out of the corner of his eye, Frank could see the round, overfed figure of Sir Muirhead bent over a table.

He risked a quick look before they reached the exit.

Then he wished he hadn't.

Because he saw, across the dining room, the cold, hard eyes of Jago Lilywhite Grace staring back at him.

Chapter Seven:
In Search of Evidence

he heavy doors swung shut behind Frank and D.K.

'Did you see them?' asked Frank.

'Who?'

'Muirhead and Jago. I saw them as we left. Muirhead was at Jago's table, talking to him. He was staring right at me.'

'Who, Muirhead?'

'No, Number One.'

A shiver went up Frank's spine as he remembered the grip of Number One's bony fingers on his wrist.

'We don't have much time', said D.K. 'If Jago has suspicions, we may find ourselves with company. He'll have a lot of people working for him. We simply don't know how big The League of the Stuffed Shirts is.'

Frank scanned the foyer. It was empty. The guests were in the ballroom, and the staff were either in the kitchens, or serving tables.

'Do you know the quickest way to the Larwood Suite from here?' asked D.K.

'Yes', said Frank. 'But maybe quickest isn't what we need right now.'

'The shortest route is past the back entrance to the kitchens. But it'll be better if we go a different way, to avoid being seen.'

'Then lead on, young man, and I will follow.'

Frank and D.K. snuck through the darkened halls of The Ancient Assembly. They crept past portraits of fearsome fast bowlers and pinch-hitting all-rounders.

They tiptoed past oil paintings of opening batters, and watercolours of wrist-spinners.

They slunk past landscapes capturing T20 six-hitting, and test match wicket-taking.

And they eventually found themselves at the entrance to the Larwood Suite.

Frank fumbled in his pocket. It was dark and quiet. They were a long way from the ballroom. The only sounds were those strange noises old buildings make when night comes round.

The Ancient Assembly of Cricket coughed and wheezed. Pipes rattled out strings of scrambled Morse code. Floorboards groaned and heaved, like the bowels of a creaking ship.

After two failed attempts, Frank extracted his security-card from his wallet and slipped it into the metal key-slot beneath the door handle.

There was a dull click, and a soft light flicked from red to green.

He turned to D.K., who gave a thumbs-up before shooing Frank inside.

The room smelt fusty and old. The memory of cigar-smoke hung in the air. It was cool, and the curtains hadn't been drawn. Empty glasses were grouped together in the middle of the table. Whoever had been on clean-up duties had only done half a job.

There was enough moonlight for Frank and D.K. to be able to see what they were doing.

Neither wanted to turn on the lights. To an outside observer, such as a security guard walking through the grounds, a single illuminated conference room, hidden away at the back of the building, would look strange.

Strange enough to encourage closer examination.

And they wanted to be left well alone while they searched.

'What are we looking for?' asked Frank, under his breath.

'I'm not sure, exactly', murmured D.K., his voice low and tight.

'Anything that might tell us who else was here with Jago and Muirhead.'

'A list or a register would be perfect, but I don't think they would keep such a thing.'

'So maybe something dropped from a pocket. A business card, perhaps. Or someone might have been forgetful, and left behind an identifying item.'

They divided the room into two halves.

Frank searched one side, D.K. the other.

They were quick. Quiet.

For D.K., it was an adventure. An exciting one. He felt new life and new energy seeping into his aging limbs.

He felt young again.

For Frank, it was more nerve-racking. He had a job he couldn't afford to lose, and a future he hadn't yet put together. For him, getting caught would lead to problems far greater than those Mr Chatterjee might face.

'Found anything?' whispered Frank who, despite careful examination of his side of the room, had failed to unearth any evidence.

D.K. shook his head.

'Nothing', he said, losing some of his enthusiasm. 'They might have swept the room before they left, to remove anything incriminating.'

'What should we do?' asked Frank, who was hoping they could leave the suite and head back to the ballroom.

No reply.

'Mr Chatterjee?' Frank hissed. 'D.K.? We need to get out of here.'

D.K. looked at Frank across the table. He placed a finger against his lips.

'Did you hear something?'

Frank held his breath and listened.

'No, I don't think so. It might have been my stomach rumbling.'*

'If only there was some kind of list', said D.K. 'A register. Number One must know the names of all the other members of the League. Would he have a list somewhere? One he uses to monitor who attends the meetings?'

Frank closed his eyes and tried to visualise the room, as it had been that morning.

He could see Number One – Jago – sitting at the head of the table.

He could see the odious Sir Muirhead Gassington tutting and harrumphing from his perch halfway down the room.

---

* In England, rumbling stomachs are a major feature of village cricket. They usually begin at around eleven in the morning, and don't quieten down until after the players have had their tea breaks. Funnily enough, the pace of play slows considerably after tea, with fast bowlers becoming slow bowlers, and many batters choosing not to run between the wickets for fear of disturbing the digestive processes hard at work in their tummies.

And he could see the other ten members of the League spaced out along both sides, each taking a copy of the contract as the pile of documents was passed around.

But he couldn't see a list of names.

Only the list he'd seen in the photocopying room ...

Number One ...

Number Two ...

Number Three ...

Then it hit him.

Hit him like a speeding yorker crashing into the toe-end of his bat.

Hit him like a short ball crunching off a top edge and rocketing over the boundary-rope for six.

The sign-in book.

The Ancient Assembly was famed the world over as an old and venerable institution. Part of its charm was the way it did things. The pace of change was slow. Memories of the past littered the building.

Pictures, paintings, memorabilia.

There were bats that had been used to nurdle the winning runs in epic test-matches.

Balls that had been used to take the final wickets in nail-biting one-day internationals.

And wicket-keeping gloves that had held the catches that ended brave T20 run-chases.

But it didn't stop there.

Some technology had been allowed into The Ancient Assembly. Such as the technology to lock and open doors using special key-cards.

But much other technology had been stopped at the gates, turned around, and politely asked to exit the area and enjoy the rest of its day.

That included electronic entry-devices.

'The sign-in book, Mr Chatterjee. That's what we need to get hold of!'

In his excitement, Frank had stopped whispering.

'Everyone has to use the sign-in book. We know what time the meeting started. So, we can work back from there. Each of them will have had to sign in. Every member of The League of the Stuffed Shirts!'

Mr Chatterjee waved his hands sharply and drew a finger to his lips.

'Brilliant, Mr Meadows', he said, his voice soft and low. 'Simply brilliant. Bravo. Now, all we need to do is get hold of the book for long enough to identify them all.'

At that moment, there was a gentle click, followed by the noise of two hands clapping in a slow, menacing rhythm.

'Congratulations, Mr Meadows. You are a more intelligent young man than I first suspected. Only, you forgot one small yet important detail.'

Jago Lilywhite Grace was standing in the doorway, his freshly-pressed tuxedo clinging to his angular, bony frame. A sneer curled his upper lip.

Light filtered into the room from the corridor.

Behind him there were three figures. The large, heavily-upholstered form of Sir Muirhead Gassington, and, on either side of him, two of the meanest, strongest-looking waiters Frank had ever seen.

Chapter Eight:
Jago's Powerplay

et me introduce you to my friends', said Jago.

'This is Dorian. He bowls at ninety miles an hour, and likes kicking people out of places where they don't belong. And this', he continued, pointing at the other waiter, 'is Ranulph. But don't let his name fool you. He holds the record for the longest six ever recorded on the playing-fields of Oxford. And he likes depositing troublemakers into bins of rotting vegetables.'

D.K. walked round the table so he could stand beside Frank.

He took his time, flicking his wrist as he went, like he was getting ready to bowl leg-spin with an invisible ball.

'I've seen the contract, Jago. I've seen it, I've read it, and I don't like it.'

'What contract?' asked Jago, smiling, his arms spread wide in mock surprise. 'You must be confused, old man.'

D.K. turned to Frank, his face asking a silent question of permission.

Frank stared straight ahead, into the uncaring eyes of Number One.

Jago continued to smile. It was a cold, icy smile. A fake smile. A smile that said a hundred things, none of them happy or warm or good.

Frank didn't like that smile. He didn't like those eyes. And he didn't like anything whatsoever about The League of the Stuffed Shirts.

He turned, looked at D.K., and saw the question his new friend was asking.

Frank nodded his agreement.

Mr Chatterjee mouthed the words 'thank you', and turned back to face Jago.

He put a hand to his bow-tie, then moved it to his moustache before drawing his fingers down in a single, long stroke. He tipped his head back, breathed in, and exhaled.

'A copy of your contract has come into my possession', he began. 'It details the activities of The League of the Stuffed Shirts.'

'What you've been up to.'

'What you are planning. And the things you intend to do to the world of cricket when – if – you gain control of OINC.'

Sir Muirhead couldn't control himself. He thrust his huge frame through the doors and was about to send the cork sailing out of the bottle when Jago spun round and grabbed hold of his nose.

'Silence, Gasbag. Silence!' he said, squeezing Sir Muirhead so hard that the knight of the realm had no choice but to lean forward and let himself be dragged about by Number One.

'The last thing any of us need is to hear your words of worthless wisdom, Gassy. Go and wait outside.'

As he finished speaking, Jago gave a sharp twist of his hand and flicked Number Six's head back towards the doors.

Sir Muirhead squealed, reached for his nose, and stumbled out of the Larwood Suite, pushing his way past Dorian and Ranulph.

'Now', said Jago, smoothing the creases in his jacket. 'Where were we?'

'Ah, yes', he continued, bringing his hands together and making a temple with his fingers. 'You say you have a copy of a contract. That is interesting.'

'As I recall from my days at law-school, a contract is a private document. It belongs to the parties who sign it. Unless, of course, they choose to share it.'

'So, I assume that you are a signatory to this contract, Mr Chatterjee? Is that not the case?'

Neither D.K. nor Frank replied.

'Well, that is interesting, isn't it? Because, if you did not sign it, then it really doesn't belong to you. Perhaps, therefore, you should return it to its rightful owner.'

'And that would be you, would it?' asked D.K. 'You are the leader of The League of the Stuffed Shirts, aren't you, Jago?'

Jago started to laugh.

It was a cruel, mocking laugh.

The kind of laugh that makes kittens cry.

'Mr Chatterjee, really. You say some extraordinary things.'

'First, you openly share your criminal activities by telling us about a stolen contract. Second, you invent some fanciful secret society with a quite ridiculous name. And third, as if that wasn't enough, you follow it up by claiming, outrageously, that I am the leader of this fictional group.'

Jago shook his head.

'If I were a different kind of person, Mr Chatterjee, I would get the police involved. I would sue you for slander. Because these are awful claims you are making. Awful. And you do not have a shred of evidence to support them.'

'We have the contract', cried Frank, who was getting angrier and angrier the more he heard Jago speak.

'And I saw you all in here.'

'All of you.'

'Twelve members of The League of the Stuffed Shirts.'

'You signed it. You agreed it. You had me be a witness. Even though I had no idea what you were doing.'

Jago moved further into the room. He tilted his head back, so he was looking down his nose at Frank.

'Have you considered what it will be like, Mr Meadows, spending the next fifty years of your life chiselling dried dog muck off pavements? Emptying buckets of kitchen waste into vast, stinking wheelie-bins. Digging manure into municipal flowerbeds. Because those are the only jobs that will be left when I've finished with you.'

'And you won't have your beloved cricket to look forward to. I will make sure you're banned from playing ever again. Every cricket pitch in England will be out of bounds.'

'And should you ever save enough money to make a trip abroad — which I doubt you will — then you'll find the cricket pitches of the world will fold their arms and turn you away.'

'We have evidence', shouted Frank. 'And we'll use it to show everybody what you're up to. The whole of cricket will know your plan, and that will be the end of you. Permanently.'

Jago tilted his head to one side.

'Evidence, you say? What evidence?'

D.K. put his arm out and signalled to Frank that he should keep quiet.

Frank could feel the blood pounding in his ears.

'Let us review the evidence, shall we?'

'First, you have a stolen copy of a contract. You claim that the contract was signed by me and some other people.'

'But a funny feeling tells me that my name isn't on the contract.'

'And it would not surprise me if this so-called contract turns out to contain no names at all.'

'Oh, you might tell me that it has signatures. But signatures can be forged, can't they?'

'And so often, a signature is very hard to read. So hard, that it could belong to a great many people.'

'And then there was your wonderful brainwave, wasn't there, Frank. The sign-in book.'

'The *famous* sign-in book.'

'A large, leather-bound book with crinkling pages. A book so big and heavy that it is hard to lift. A book known around the world as the Record-Keeper. A history of the comings and goings at The Ancient Assembly of Cricket. With entries covering more than a century of cricketing times gone by.'

'Your plan is to look in the book and identify who was in this room earlier today. I heard you through the doors, Frank. A fine plan, I'm sure.'

'Only, there's a small problem. A tiny detail you forgot to consider.'

'That book was severely damaged in a freak accident. Damaged so badly that the most recent pages could not be saved. Isn't that right, Dorian?'

The hulking fast bowler shifted his weight from one foot to the other.

'Yes, Mr Grace, terrible accident.'

'And you know, the funny thing is, something tells me this accident is going to take place in the next few minutes. Isn't that right, Dorian?'

Frank looked from Jago to Dorian and back again.

'Yes, Mr Grace. I'll just go off to reception now and make sure it happens at the right time.'

Jago clapped his hands together.

'Wonderful to have such forward-thinking staff, isn't it, Mr Chatterjee?'

D.K. did not reply. He employed a very different kind of person to Dorian. And he treated them very differently as well.

'So, let me summarise the situation.'

'You two are involved in a criminal conspiracy. You have conspired together to steal a contract. You claim I am somehow connected to this contract, yet you have no evidence. You left the gala dinner to go sneaking round the building.'

'And you, Mr Meadows, abused the trust of your employers.'

'You used your key-card to get into this room illegally.'

'And you helped a man who, while highly respected in the world of cricket, has no business snooping through the hallowed corridors of this cricketing sanctuary.'

'I can really only see one way forward. I will have to report you, Mr Meadows. First to the police, then to your employer.'

'You will lose your job. Of that, I am sure. And who knows what else? Maybe your freedom too. I hear prison food is not what it once was.'

Jago Lilywhite Grace took a deep breath.

He smoothed down the hair on the side of his head, then dusted each arm of his jacket.

'There is one alternative, I suppose', he said, tossing the words out as if he were throwing bits of stale bread to ducks in a pond.

'One means of escape.'

He straightened his fingers, held his hands in front of himself and inspected his fingernails.

'You give me the contract. And I forget any of this ever happened.'

Chapter Nine:
Mr Chatterjee Leads
the Counterattack

rank opened his mouth, ready to speak.

Jago put a finger to his lips and made a shushing sound.

'I love listening to monkeys, Mr Meadows, but only at the zoo. I'll listen to the organ-grinder this time, I think. Chatterjee, what do you say?'

Frank clenched his fingers into a fist and bit his lip.

How he'd love to get his hands on this Jago character. Even better, how he'd love to face him on a cricket pitch. He didn't bowl much these days, but he was sure he'd be able to send down an over of rip-snorting fast bowling if Jago Lilywhite Grace was padded up and taking guard.

D.K. shrugged his shoulders, then smoothed the fabric of his jacket.

He reached a hand to his neck and tugged lightly at his bow-tie, pulling it straight.

'A lovely speech, Mr Grace. You have always been a conjuror with words, if not with your bat.'

Behind Jago, the barrel-like figure of Ranulph edged forwards.

Number One raised a hand, signalling that this was not the time for an intervention of the physical kind.

D.K. continued. 'I say a contract exists, and that you signed it. You deny this.'

'Yet, in the same breath, you tell me that I should hand over the contract.'

'Now, didn't you yourself say that a contract is a private matter? That it belongs to those who signed it?'

'Is that not what Mr Grace said, Frank? You heard him, didn't you?'

'Yes', said Frank, his voice firm. 'He definitely said it.'

'Good, good', said D.K.

'So, I can only assume, Mr Grace, that if you are demanding I hand over the contract, it is because the contract belongs to you. And it can only belong to you if you signed it. Isn't that right?'

Jago screwed up his face.

The icy smile transformed into a look of hatred.

There was a clicking sound as he flexed his jaw.

His shoulders hunched inwards. He tapped his fingers together, tips to tips.

Behind him, Ranulph waited, rocking on the balls of his feet, ready for instructions.

None came.

Frank marvelled at Mr Chatterjee's skilful handling of the situation. It was like watching a seam bowler extract reverse swing from a flat batting track.

Jago was wrong-footed. He was flailing at the unexpected movements of the ball. Unable to understand where it was going, and why he could no longer hit it.

'Are you the monkey, Mr Grace, or the organ-grinder? Only, I don't seem to be hearing from either at the moment. You've gone so quiet.'

D.K. knew what he was doing. Goading a man like Grace was a further attempt to put him off-balance. To tip the advantage back in their favour.

Jago grinned.

Frank could make out the faintest sliver of white peeking from between his lips.

Number One spoke slowly, weighing his words.

'Very good, Mr Chatterjee. Very good. I can see how you have amassed your fortune. Not much gets past you.'

'Still, it matters not.'

'You are too late to do anything. The wheels were set in motion long before Mr Meadows grubbed his nose into business that does not concern him.'

'Shortly, I will be elected as the new leader of OINC. And I feel sure that some of my closest associates will also find themselves selected for positions of power within the cricketing world.'

'And then ...'

He turned his gaze from Frank to D.K. and back again. A spider, deciding which fly looked the juiciest.

'Then the world of cricket will be cleansed of the likes of you. It will be made into what it has always needed to be. Something pure. Something elite. Something controlled.'

'A sport with boundaries. Boundaries that prevent riff-raff from ruining it.'

He spat the word 'riff-raff' out of his mouth like it was a bad taste he was trying to get rid of.

'Keep the contract, gentlemen, if you really have it. You can't use it, because then you will have to explain how you stole it. And you have no evidence that it is real. No one will believe you. Worse, they will question your motives.'

'They will say you are jealous. Envious. We all know that you were thwarted in your attempts to get onto the board of OINC, Chatterjee.'

'People will look at you, brandishing a stolen contract containing no names, given to you by an idiotic man-child who dusts windows for a living, and conclude what I concluded a long time ago.'

'That you, Chatterjee, are a loser.'

'Face it, gentlemen, you have arrived late to the game, tried to play your shots, and failed miserably.'

Jago flicked his hand at Frank and D.K. It was like he was flicking them away, out of his life. As if they were a pair of raindrops he was brushing from his windscreen.

He turned, clicked his fingers at Ranulph, and pointed to the corridor.

Sir Muirhead Gassington, who had been loitering outside the Larwood Suite, started to speak.

Jago silenced him with an imperious sweep of his hand.

Already he was preparing for his role as the emperor of cricket. The role he had imagined for himself.

The role he was now in the process of bringing to life.

'How are those bats working out for you, Mr Grace?'

It was D.K., his voice calm and level.

Frank watched as Jago stopped a couple of paces before the open doors.

He tipped his head to one side but did not turn around.

'I've been thinking about changing my supplier', he said. 'I've heard some terrible stories about my current one.'

'That's interesting, Mr Grace', said D.K. 'very interesting.'

'Only this afternoon I was reviewing our contract. It's amazing how many times you have to sign these things, isn't it? One signature here, one signature there. Page after page with your signature.'

'Page after page with my signature. Quite incredible really, when you think about it. All those signatures. All so similar. Identical even. Every one of mine looks the same. And every one of yours looks the same as well.'

'I guess that's what happens, isn't it? The more people sign their name, the less variation there is. It gets to a point when your signature comes out the same every time. Down to the smallest marks.'

Frank was listening intently.

He remembered practising his own signature as a child.

Writing his name again and again and again.

Filling sheets of paper, the inside cover of his exercise book, even a corner of the kitchen table.

'And then we have this other contract, don't we, Mr Grace? Containing twelve signatures. Ten I'm not too sure about, though I could make some educated guesses.'

'But two I recognise clearly.'

'Two are familiar to me.'

'They are signatures I have seen many times; on contracts I have also signed.'

'Because one is your signature, Mr Grace. And the other belongs to our mutual friend. The friend who has joined us here this evening. Isn't that right, Sir Muirhead?'

The knight of the realm shook his head and muttered. His jowls wobbled along, echoing his disagreement.

'You can't prove anything, Chatterjee', he said, without conviction.

'Oh, but I can', said D.K.

'I can provide irrefutable evidence that those signatures belong to the pair of you. Evidence so strong that it could not have been forged or made up.'

'Evidence that shows an exact match between the signatures used in this room earlier today, and the signatures on the contracts I possess.'

'Contracts to supply bats and cricket equipment to companies owned by you, Mr Grace, and you, Sir Muirhead.'

Frank watched Jago. He was listening: you could see that in his body. Listening with great care and attention. He was like a statue. Unmoving. His back still facing Mr Chatterjee.

A moment went past.

Then another.

Then Frank saw Number One gesture to Ranulph and Sir Muirhead that they should wait outside, in the corridor.

And, finally, after the doors clicked shut, he turned round.

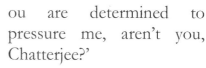

Chapter Ten:
A Deal is Struck

ou are determined to pressure me, aren't you, Chatterjee?'

Jago clasped his hands together and rested his index fingers on his lips.

'You think you are a fast bowler who can intimidate a batter with short-pitched deliveries.'

'You will discover, Mr Chatterjee, that I can hook and pull as well as anybody.'

Jago advanced across the space between the two of them.

Frank instinctively moved closer to D.K. He was ready to face up to Jago and push him back – if that was required.

'Calm down, Mr Meadows', said Jago. 'I have no desire to spill blood on this white shirt of mine.'

'Why can't you just leave things the way they are?' said Frank. 'Why do you have to be so horrible? Cricket is a game for everybody, not just the few.'

D.K. looked at Frank, then back at Jago.

'The innocence of youth speaks truths forgotten by old men', he said.

Jago scoffed.

'Did you get that from a fortune cookie, Chatterjee?'

'Or maybe you have it written on a piece of wood stuck to the wall of your kitchen.'

He flicked his head up.

'What rot', he said.

'And what do you know of life, Mr Meadows?'

'You are scarcely older than a child, and you spend your days removing dust from paintings of men whose skills and exploits you will never match.'

'The very problem we face is that the future of cricket has been shaped by idiots like you.'

'Go ahead and share your copy of the contract.'

'What do I care? I will simply tell people that it is an elaborate forgery. Then I will tie you up in so many legal knots that you'll feel like a piece of rigging on a tall ship.'

'It will take years, and a great deal of money, to free yourself from the web my lawyers will create. And by then I will have brought the world of cricket to heel.'

'The plebs – that is, people like you two – will be grateful they are allowed to watch from the side-lines. While the true elite, the aristocrats of the game, will grace the fields of green with their presence.'*

For a few moments, Jago stood there, staring at Frank. His eyes were narrow, and his chin jutted forward. His breathing was slow yet loud, like he was struggling to control it.

'Maybe what you say is true', said D.K., choosing his words with care. 'But if I release my copy of the contract, along with my evidence about your signature, there will inevitably be questions.'

'And questions make people talk. And when people start talking, it is hard to stop them.'

'Oh, you might be able to muddy the waters, Mr Grace, with the help of your lawyers. But enough people will believe my side of the story to make life difficult for you.'

Jago's nose twitched, and he bared his teeth.

'What you really want, despite what you say, is for this contract to remain a secret.'

'For it to never see the light of day.'

---

* Aristocrats are not to be confused with aristocats. Aristocrats are rich and wealthy people, often with names like Lord Ponsonby-Smythe and The Marquis of Bogsworth. Whereas aristocats are cats who think they are better than everyone else. Which covers a lot of cats.

'And I just might know a way I can make that happen for you.'

Mr Chatterjee's words almost knocked Frank over.

He couldn't believe what he was hearing.

After everything D.K. had said, was he now offering to help Jago? Had he switched sides? Was he going to hand Frank over to his doom, without so much as a warning?

The atmosphere in the room changed.

Jago relaxed, took a step back.

Mr Chatterjee smiled.

A thaw was developing, the ice melting away.

Frank started to wonder whether Mr Chatterjee had given up hope.

Did he think there was no way of stopping Number One from altering the world of cricket forever?

Or, worse, had he decided to throw his lot in with Jago, and become the thirteenth member of the League?

He looked on, his mouth open, trying to understand what was happening. Trying to unravel the game these two powerful men were playing in front of him.

'Are you a gambling man, Mr Grace?'

Jago rubbed his hands together.

'On occasion, Mr Chatterjee, if I like the odds.'

'I propose a bet. A gamble. A way of dealing with this … difficult situation.'

'As I see it, we want different things.'

'You, Mr Grace, want my copy of the contract, and my silence.'

'I, on the other hand, want to stop your plan, and to put an end to this League of the Stuffed Shirts you have formed.'

'The problem is that these things do not go together. They cannot both happen. Only one.'

'And, if neither of us gets what we want, it will cause problems for us both.'

'So, I propose a wager. A sporting wager. Between two cricket lovers.'

'After all, while we might see the future of the game differently, we do at least share a love for it. Is that not true, Mr Grace?'

Jago was weighing every word he heard. Scrutinising sentences. Scanning for traps.

'Go on, Mr Chatterjee. I'm listening.'

'My proposal is this. A cricket match. Rules to be decided. Two teams. Yours and mine. No professionals. All players to be eighteen years of age or younger.'

'If you win, I will destroy my copy of the contract.'

'If I win, you will give up your position as Governor of OINC and disband The League of the Stuffed Shirts.'

'That is the wager. Let us settle this on the field of play.'

Mr Chatterjee waited a moment, then leaned forward.

'The question is, Mr Grace, do you have the bottle?'

Jago licked his lips, then bared his teeth.

'Oh yes, Mr Chatterjee. I have the bottle all right. And I will have the players to grind your team into the dust.'

'So, we have a deal?' asked D.K.

'Almost', replied Jago. 'There are three questions I need answering. First, when will this match take place?'

D.K. glanced at Frank, who looked like he was at a crossroads with a sat nav that had started speaking Martian.

'Six months from now. That will give us both time to select a team and to coach them.'

'Fine. Question two. Where will this match be played?'

'Here. At The Ancient Assembly of Cricket. We will call it the Governor's Invitational. A match to mark the start of your leadership of OINC. Or to signal its end.'

Jago shook his head.

'You will spend the next six months deluding yourself that you have a chance, Chatterjee.'

Number One pointed a bony finger in Frank's direction.

'Question three. What about Mr Meadows?'

His voice changed as he said Frank's name. He spat the words from his mouth.

'What about him?' asked D.K. 'I don't see that Frank has anything to do with the wager.'

'Ah, but he does, Mr Chatterjee, he does.'

'You see, Mr Meadows is the start of this story.'

'He is the one who stole a copy of the contract.

'He is the one who brought it to you.'

'He is the one who wishes to see me unseated from my throne.'

'How can I be certain he won't go blabbing to the newspapers in the next six months?'

'How can I be sure he won't reveal all he knows before the match, and ruin the bet?'

D.K. looked at Frank.

'Mr Meadows? Can we trust you to remain silent on this matter?'

A terrible feeling of uncertainty swept through Frank's stomach.

His left foot was twitching. Sweat clung to his brow.

Reluctantly, he nodded.

'Yes', he said, his mouth dry. 'If that's what you want, Mr Chatterjee, I'll do it.'

'Wonderful', said Jago. There was sarcasm in his voice.

'So, all I have to rely on is the word of a thief. Not good enough, Chatterjee.'

'This drinks-fetcher needs to be put out of the picture. Transported to the other side of the world and prevented from speaking to anyone about anything for the next six months.'

Frank's face went red.

'Just you try it!' he shouted. 'I'll knock you for six!'

'A. Very. Loose. Cannon.' said Jago, smirking. 'He is a deal-breaker, I'm afraid.'

'Do not concern yourself with Mr Meadows', said D.K. 'I will personally vouch for him.'

'And I will take him into my employ for the next six months. He will be by my side and in my confidence. If he reveals anything about the contract, the League, or our wager, I will forfeit, and you will be victorious.'

'Is that all right with you, Mr Meadows?'

Frank looked around.

Strangely, the first thing that came into his head was a question.

Where would he practice if he couldn't use the facilities at The Ancient Assembly?

That was followed by another.

Would Mr Chatterjee pay him, and what would he expect him to do?

'Drinks-fetcher', cooed Jago. 'We need an answer.'

Frank was lost in his thoughts.

He blinked, saw Jago staring at him, then pulled at his shirt collar.

He was sure the room was getting warmer.

'Uh-huh', he said.

'Speak up, carpet-sweeper, we can't hear you.'

'Yes. It's all right. I'll do it.'

'Thank you, Frank', said D.K., giving a little bow of respect as he spoke.

'We have a deal, Jago?'

'We do', said Number One, the head of The League of the Stuffed Shirts, and the soon-to-be-appointed Governor of OINC. 'Now let us shake on it.'

Frank watched as the two men came together.

As they shook hands, he thought he could see a thousand careful calculations being made behind Jago's eyes, and he didn't like it one bit.

Chapter Eleven:
An Enterprise is Agreed

he hands of the clock stood at well past midnight.

Frank and D.K. sat in two large leather armchairs in Mr Chatterjee's mansion flat.

They had their bow-ties and top buttons undone, and were drinking cups of hot, sweet tea.

After the deal was made, the five of them – Frank, D.K., Jago, Ranulph, and Sir Muirhead – returned to the gala dinner, in time for the main course.

Dorian joined them shortly after, winking at Jago as he served his master's lamb-shank with mashed potatoes and green beans.

The rest of the evening was uneventful. Election results were announced. To little surprise, Sir Muirhead was appointed as an OINC board member, along with half a dozen others.

It was then declared that Jago Lilywhite Grace had been successful in his campaign to become Governor. After the six-month hand-over period, he would succeed the current Governor, Sanath Perera.

Frank had to bite his tongue while he listened to Jago's acceptance speech.

He'd never heard so much rubbish in all his life.

'We're agreed?'

'Yes.'

'Good. I'm sorry you had to become a part of all this, Frank.'

'But I admire your bravery, and how you have risen to a test that has been thrown your way.'

'I can see why you have such fine prospects as a batter. You do not recognise defeat — only the opportunity to accept a new challenge.'

Frank smiled, and took a sip of his tea.

'In the morning I will provide you with the address of my nephew, along with enough money to cover all your expenses.'

'You will take the train to Manchester, find him, and then begin your search.'

'I will speak to him before your arrival, to explain the situation.'

'It's a good plan, Mr Chatterjee. It gives us a fighting chance.'

D.K. rose from his chair and raised his cup.

Frank did the same.

'To our enterprise, Mr Meadows. And to our success!'

As their cups clinked together, both felt a mixture of fear and excitement at the thought of the bet they had made with Jago.

Fear at the possibility of losing.

Excitement at the thought of winning.

The stakes were high.

The game was afoot!

They were in it.

And they had a fighting chance.

A beeping noise told everyone that the train doors were closing.

Frank sat beside a window, wearing a hoody and a pair of jeans.

As the train pulled out of Euston Station, he went over the plan in his mind.

Throughout the gala dinner, after the meeting with Jago, D.K. had been plotting what they would do.

Back at the mansion flat he had explained it all to Frank.

It went something like this:

They needed to put a team together. And not just any team. An incredible team. A team of all the talents. A team composed of the best, most exciting young cricketers around.

Not only that, but this team had to be international. It needed cricketers from across the world. From different backgrounds. From different places.

It had to prove to Jago, and to everyone else in The League of the Stuffed Shirts, that cricket was for everybody. That cricket was better when it was open, and free, and accessible to all.

D.K. would stay in London.

He had to try to discover who else was in the League. Which other ten members of the cricketing world were conspiring with Jago and Sir Muirhead to raise the drawbridge and control entry to the game.

Frank would need to travel. He was the one who would have to put the team together, with D.K.'s help.

Mr Chatterjee had factories all over the world. Homes too.

He was wealthy and well-connected.

He was known by cricketers on every continent.

As well as searching for the other members of the League, he would tap into his network of contacts. Carefully, though — so as not to arouse suspicion.

It was not lost on either of them that anyone could be a member of the League.

Anyone at all.

He would use his network to unearth some of the finest young cricketers there were. It would then be up to Frank to find these cricketers, to talk to them, and to convince them to join the team.

They had six months; but ideally, they would use the last month for training and coaching.

And there, Frank would also be expected to take the lead.

D.K. knew that he was a quality batter.

Now, after the events that had transpired the previous evening, he had seen up close how Frank responded to a challenge.

It was enough to persuade him that the young Mr Meadows had what it took to coach the team, as well as locate the players.

So Frank was on his way to Manchester, and their enterprise had begun.

Mr Chatterjee's nephew, Virender, awaited him.

He was working in one of his uncle's bat-making factories, learning the family business.

Close in age to Frank, he was also a cricketer. A fast bowler.

Frank would meet with Virender, and together they would search for the first cricketer Mr Chatterjee had discovered.

A young boy known locally as The Stump Smasher.

A few months earlier, Mr Chatterjee had been in conversation with one of the managers of the Manchester factory.

These conversations focused less on bat production and more on what was happening in the world of cricket.

And D.K. was as interested in local happenings as he was in international ones.

The manager had told him of a rumour that was doing the rounds in the northern leagues.

It was said that there was a young fast bowler, still in school, who was bowling rockets so fast and accurate that they were sending shockwaves through the county.

Off stumps were cartwheeling across the grass.

Middle stumps were soaring into the air.

And leg stumps were careering off towards the boundary.

The manager told Mr Chatterjee that the young bowler was so feared by the local batters that they had started calling him the Stump Smasher.

Some said he was as fast as Dennis Lillee and Jeff Thomson put together.[*]

Others said he rivalled the West Indian fast bowlers of the 1970s and 1980s: Andy Roberts, Colin Croft, Michael Holding, Malcolm Marshall and Joel Garner.[†]

---

[*] Lillee and Thomson were the most fearsome Australian fast-bowling duo of the 1970s. In 1976, both Lillee and Thomson were recorded bowling balls at over 95 miles per hour. Which is almost twice as fast as a lion running at top speed.

[†] Five of the fastest, smartest and most skilful bowlers who have ever played. They were part of the West Indian team that dominated test cricket throughout the late 1970s and the entire 1980s. A team that many people regard as the greatest of all time.

And everyone agreed that they preferred playing on the days when he had to stay in and do his homework.

Frank looked out of the window.

The green fields and tidy gardens of suburban England whizzed past.

He hoped that the rumours about The Stump Smasher were true. And he hoped he would be able to convince him to be the first member of his and D.K.'s team.

A team they didn't have a name for.

A team that currently had zero players.

And a team that needed to take shape pretty quickly if they were going to have a chance of beating Jago, and defeating The League of the Stuffed Shirts.

Chapter Twelve:
To Walk or Not To Walk

rank woke up.

Streams of people were passing beside the train.

Behind them, he could see a sign reading: 'Welcome to Manchester'.

He rubbed his eyes, pulled himself out of his seat, and stretched. Reaching up, he took his bag from the luggage rack.

On the platform he felt the cool morning air hit his face.

A voice was speaking over the tannoy, telling everyone who was interested that the 10.03 to Leeds was now ready to depart.

Frank rested his bag on the floor, next to an information board.

D.K. had given him instructions on how to reach the Chatterjee bat factory. He took the printed map from his jeans pocket and ran his finger along the route.

It was a fifty-minute walk, or a fifteen-minute taxi ride.

Yesterday, he would have walked, no question.

Today, he had a wallet full of petty cash to cover his expenses. The most money he had ever seen in his life.

Mr Chatterjee had pulled a wad of notes out of his safe and handed them to Frank, and at the same time he'd placed the copy of the contract inside the safe.

Frank decided he would buy himself some breakfast and then find a taxi. The driver would have no trouble getting him to the factory, and Virender knew he was coming.

He passed through the ticket gate and saw a bright, welcoming coffee-shop selling pastries and sandwiches.

As he walked towards it, he thought the start of his mission was going very smoothly indeed, all things considered.

This whole business would probably turn out to be a doddle. Much easier than he had first assumed.

D.K. would find the players, and Frank would pick them up from the four corners of the globe.

And at the end of it, they would give Jago's team a thrashing, and put a stop to The League of the Stuffed Shirts once and for all.

It was the last time that these kinds of thoughts would swim lazily through Frank's mind.

But he didn't know that.

Not yet anyway.

Frank leaned back in his seat.

Something didn't feel right.

He'd eaten his croissant and drunk his coffee.

Both had been good.

The café was deserted. He was sitting by the window, facing into the shop.

Two baristas, a man and a woman not much older than he was, were chatting to each other behind the counter.*

It was quiet. The morning rush had ended. It wouldn't be busy again until lunchtime.

Frank fished the map from his pocket and smoothed it out on the table.

He felt less sure of himself now. And more anxious.

Maybe it was the coffee.

He was no longer convinced that getting a taxi was the right option.

---

* A barista is someone who has mastered the art of making coffee. They shouldn't be confused with a barrister, who is a lawyer who has mastered the art of speaking to a judge and jury. Many a case has been lost by an unwitting defendant employing a barista to defend them in court. While many awful cups of coffee have been produced by unemployed barristers working in coffee shops.

Walking might be better.

It was good exercise.

And it would give him time to think about what he would say to The Stump Smasher when he found him.

As he deliberated over the best course of action, he noticed the baristas raising their voices.

He looked up and saw them both gesturing towards the window.

Automatically, he turned to where they were pointing, and saw what they had seen.

A lady in a long, patterned coat was trying to untangle her dog lead from a ticket gate. She was waving her arms around and shouting for help.

The dog, small and wiry, sat patiently on the other side of the gate, wondering what all the fuss was about.

'I'll go and get a guard for her', said the male barista. 'They're probably off chatting somewhere.'

Frank watched him exit the coffee-shop and walk towards the lady dog-owner. The barista was tall, with a dark beard and curly brown hair. His uniform was a little on the big side. It hung off him, the t-shirt rippling as he walked.

Following him with his eyes, Frank wondered why there were no guards near the gates.

And then he froze.

All thoughts of guards and dogs and baristas were wiped from his mind.

His shoulders tightened.

He felt a tremor run through his legs like a bolt of lightning speeding its way from the sky to the earth.

Sitting on a bench halfway across the concourse, partially hidden behind a bank of ticket machines, was a large, muscular young man wearing dark glasses, a brown double-breasted raincoat, and a tweed cap.

Despite the disguise, Frank knew who it was.

Dorian.

Jago's very own pet.

And he was off his leash.

He looked like he'd taken fashion advice from a bad spy film.

On another day, at another time, it might have been funny. But Frank couldn't find much to laugh about.

A shiver ran along his shoulders.

Jago must have sent him.

And that meant that Jago and his henchmen had been watching Frank since the previous night.

Without realising, he started tapping his foot on the hard wooden floor.

'So that was how it was going to be, was it?' he thought.

Jago Lilywhite Grace wasn't the kind of person who was prepared to play the game the right way.

That much was clear.

He should have known. Should have guessed that it wouldn't be as easy as it had first seemed.

Already, Jago had shown his hand. And it didn't look good for Frank.

Or for D.K., for that matter.

Now he knew that Jago would be doing his level best to make life difficult for both of them.

And that might include trying to poach the players D.K. had identified.

Or even preventing Frank from getting to those players in the first place.

Dorian was looking in Frank's direction.

His dark glasses obscured his eyes.

Frank stood up, threw his bag over his shoulder, and walked out of the café.

He turned left as soon as he was on the concourse, rounded a corner and knelt beside a wall, pretending to tie his shoelace.

He counted.

One, two, three …

Fifteen, sixteen, seventeen …

Twenty-four, twenty-five …

On the next beat, a brown raincoat and a pair of black shoes swept past him.

Holding his breath, he risked a glance, and saw Dorian walking towards the taxi rank, coat swishing with each stride.

He watched as the badly-dressed spy exited the station.

Frank was tense, his body primed to run.

He could feel his heart beating, and moisture on his palms.

The first car at the rank began to pull away.

Dorian ran towards it, but it was already accelerating.

Frank watched him jerk open the door of a second cab, bundle himself inside it, and slam the door shut, while barking instructions at the driver and jabbing a finger.

As Frank stood up, there was a split-second in which he thought he saw Dorian turn his head and look back inside the station.

But he couldn't be certain.

This was bad news.

If Dorian had followed him to Manchester, how many other henchmen might be on his tail?

Jago had money, power, and connections. On top of that, he had the resources of The League of the Stuffed Shirts at his disposal.

Frank would have to be careful.

He would have to focus.

It would be like opening the batting in a test match. Maximum concentration. Eyes alert. Scanning his surroundings. Making sure he knew where his stumps were, and how best to protect them. Making sure he didn't succumb to any silly mistakes and throw everything away.

If Dorian had seen him, he would now be arguing with the taxi driver, telling him to turn round and go back to the station.

A relaxing taxi journey through Manchester would have to wait for another day.

It would be safer to walk.

Frank flipped his hood over his head, tightened the straps of his backpack, and set off in the opposite direction to the taxi rank, into the busy streets of Manchester city centre.

Chapter Thirteen: Time to Run

He tried to blend in.

He was a young man on his way to work, he told himself. Or a student off to college. That was what people would think when they saw him.

If Dorian or any other of Jago's puppets were stalking the streets of Manchester, they would struggle to pick him out.

He walked through the city centre, trying to move quickly, but not so quickly as to draw attention.

It was packed.

People milled around. Men and women, girls and boys. Tourists, workers, and schoolchildren out on trips. Trams came, arrived, and pulled away. Cars tooted their horns, and bikes whizzed along cycle-lanes.

He passed bright shop windows filled with clothes and books and furniture. He could smell bread baking, and bacon being grilled.

The scent of soap tugged at his nostrils, swirling out of doorways, curling around handwritten blackboards encouraging people to step inside, so they could open their wallets and purses and hand over their cash.

A couple of times he stopped to check the map.

And to see if he could tell whether he was being followed.

It wasn't long before he found himself slipping beyond the edges of the city centre.

The shops started to disappear.

And so did the people, the noise, and the smells.

Before he knew it, he was on a quiet road stacked on either side with flats and office blocks.

A few cars drove past, some leaving town, some heading towards it. But other than that, he was alone. No one else was on foot, walking the pavements like he was.

He checked the map again.

This was the right way. He was sure of it.

There was a bridge ahead, over a river.

He needed to cross that, continue for another mile, and then he would be there.

One more look at the map, to be certain. It had to be the right way.

Was his mind starting to play tricks on him?

This was exactly what Jago would have wanted. To knock him off his game. Sow the seeds of doubt. Make him question his decisions. Draw him into playing a false shot.

It *was* the right way. He knew it was. He told himself it was.

Having crossed the bridge, he looked along the road ahead.

It was straight and unbending.

At the end was a T-junction, with a set of traffic lights.

He felt exposed. He felt like he stuck out. There was no one walking nearby. He was alone.

A bus went past.

Then, a few seconds later, a taxi.

He jumped.

It was the first taxi he'd seen since leaving the city centre.

Travelling fast, it raced away, pushing the speed limit.

Then two square patches of red appeared. A pair of angry eyes looking back at him.

Brake-lights.

The taxi was about fifty metres ahead when it came to a halt.

Frank pulled his hood further over his face, crossed the street and jogged towards a bus shelter.

He sat down, slouching into the hard plastic seat.

The passenger door of the taxicab swung open.

Frank watched as a figure emerged.

Dorian.

This was the last thing he needed.

The hulking monolith was starting to get on his nerves.

He was ridiculous in his charity-shop spy get-up. But dangerous as well.

The taxi drove away, leaving Dorian standing on the pavement, looking up and down the street.

Frank watched him take a map from his pocket.

He saw him remove his sunglasses and bring the map closer to his face.

He watched him scratch his head and hold the map at arm's length.

Then he saw Dorian turn the map one hundred and eighty degrees.

He'd been looking at it upside down!

Maybe Dorian wasn't as smart as he was strong.

But why would he be out here with a map? At the station, it looked like he was following Frank. So, what would he be using a map for?

Then it dawned on him.

Dorian already knew where Frank was heading. The League of the Stuffed Shirts knew D.K.'s plan. Or, at least, the first part of it.

They must have guessed that Frank's trip to Manchester would involve his making a beeline for the Chatterjee bat factory.*

And what would Dorian do if he got there first? Could he try to steal information about The Stump Smasher? Or would he find Virender, and tell him a pack of lies that turned him against Frank?

Jago was not someone who would play by the rules. Not unless they were set in his favour. Frank could see that now.

Dorian was Jago's insurance policy.

Designed to stop Frank getting to The Stump Smasher.

Intended to prevent him from persuading the hottest prospect in the Lancashire leagues that joining the team he and D.K. were putting together was ideal for him.

There was only one thing for it. Frank would have to make sure he arrived at the factory before Dorian.

Nothing could get in his way.

Nothing could stop him.

---

* A beeline is very different to a line of bees. If you see a line of bees, try joining the back of it. You never know, they might be queuing for something interesting.

The consequences were too great.

He couldn't let D.K. down. The whole of cricket was relying on the pair of them: yet nobody even knew this.

He sprang from the thin plastic seat of the bus shelter, hit the ground, and started running.

Frank was a good runner. He ran long distances to keep fit. And he practiced shuttle runs so he could race between the wickets when he was at the crease.

Stealing a second run was one of his favourite things to do while batting. He could turn ones into twos, and twos into threes.*

It was an important part of his game. And he hoped it would serve him well now.

Dorian looked up from his map.

He didn't like Manchester. It smelled funny, and the people had strange accents.

It wasn't the same as London. There was no underground, and the road signs were confusing.

Then there were the peculiar things you saw.

---

* Former India captain, and all-time great, Virat Kohli, speeds between the wickets at an incredible pace. He doesn't just play fabulous shots in all forms of the game, but knows the importance of putting pressure on the fielders and picking up extra runs wherever possible. The only limit on his running is if the other batters can't keep up with him!

At the station, he'd watched a lady and a dog trap themselves in a ticket gate. And here, there was a student crossing the road, sitting down at a bus stop, then getting up again and running off at top speed, in the opposite direction to the bus!

He'd heard stories about northerners from his father. Many seemed to involve whippets, flat caps, and enormous servings of gravy.

They were an odd bunch.

Probably stupid as well, most of them, if this student was anything to go by.

What kind of idiot runs away from a bus stop?

He put on his sunglasses, adjusted his tweed cap, tightened the belt on his double-breasted overcoat, and started walking in the direction of the city centre.

Then he paused, took the map from his pocket, looked at it, folded it up, unfolded it, and flipped it over.

After a few minutes scratching his ear, he turned around and started walking in the opposite direction, hoping that no one had noticed his mistake.

The Chatterjee bat factory couldn't be far away.

It would be a relief when he'd completed his mission and could go back home.

His stomach was grumbling. It was a good job Jago was paying him double for this, because it wasn't much fun. Too many things to think about. It hurt his head.

He could see the traffic lights up ahead. The runner had vanished.

The Chatterjee bat factory was a large red-brick building set back from the road, with parking in front.

Above the entrance, a foundation stone carried the legend '1897', the date the building was completed.

D.K. had bought it twenty years ago, and had turned it into the most important centre of bat manufacturing in the north of England.

On the roof a set of big, white letters trimmed with gold spelled out 'Chatterjee's Bats'.

It was like the 'Hollywood' sign, only with more cricket involved.

The 't's' were made from specially manufactured cricket bats. A large vertical one and a smaller horizontal one. And the apostrophe was a big, red, oversized cricket ball.

The car park was full. The factory employed a lot of people and kept long hours.

Chatterjee bats were in high demand. Everybody wanted one. Children and adults

across the country liked nothing more than to hear the sweet sound of a cricket ball thwacking off the middle of a Blastmaster 2000.*

It was in Manchester, in this very factory, that the Blastmaster 2000 had been born. A bat now used in T20 leagues around the world, by batters young and old, novices and masters. It was famed for its perfect balance, and the amount of power concentrated in its middle.

A new six-hitting distance record was established not long after it went on sale. And the record had been broken five times since.

When Frank arrived at the entrance, he was sweating.

He paused, took a moment to catch his breath, looked over his shoulder, flipped his hood down, and went inside.

'Hello, sir, how may I help you?'

The smiling receptionist sat behind a dark mahogany desk. The room was like a gentleman's club, only brighter. Two huge windows let light in. The top third of each was stained glass.

The first had a design of a batter playing a forward defensive. The second showed a wicketkeeper holding a ball aloft and claiming a catch.

---

* Only a few things can be satisfactorily thwacked. A cricket ball is one of them. Chris Gayle thwacked a few in his career. In fact, he thwacked 1609 of them for six, at a rate of 1.7 sixes per innings in T20 cricket and international matches. Not bad going, eh?

Behind the receptionist there were fifty or more framed photographs, all different sizes.

Each was of a cricketer (many of them world-famous) collecting a bat from the factory.

Mr Chatterjee was in most of them, a wide grin spread across his face.

Signatures were scrawled across the pictures. Some even had messages written on them:

'The next hundred is for you.'

'Can you sand down the edges for me?'

'Nobody beats Chatterjee's!'

For a moment, caught up in the collection of images filled with cricketers he knew and loved, Frank forgot where he was, and why he was there.

'Sir?' asked the receptionist, leaning forward.

Frank shook his head.

It brought him back to reality. Brought him back to his mission.

'I'm looking for Virender', he said. 'Mr Chatterjee sent me.'

'Of course', said the receptionist. 'We've been expecting you, Mr Meadows. Did you have a pleasant journey?'

Frank raised his eyebrows.

'It was eventful', he said.

Chapter Fourteen: Sir Viv

'm Virender: how do you do?'

'Call me Viv. Everyone does. You must be Frank. Great to meet you. My uncle rang first thing this morning. Well, he's not really my uncle. Actually, he's my great uncle. But that doesn't matter, does it?

'It's Virender Ishan Vivek Chatterjee, you see. V.I.V. Chatterjee. Viv. Like Sir Viv. Viv Richards. I.V.A. Richards.

'One of the greatest batters of all time. The Master Blaster.'*

Frank nodded enthusiastically.

---

* There have been few better batters in the history of cricket than Sir Vivian Richards. He scored over 8,000 test match runs at an average of more than 50. Across his career, in total he scored more than 36,000 runs, including over a hundred centuries. He was famed for his aggressive, attacking batting that helped win many matches for all the sides he played for. He captained the West Indies from 1984 to 1991, in fifty test matches. And he never lost a test series. He won the 1975 and 1979 Cricket World Cups, playing a key role in both finals, including a century in the 1979 final. In 1976 he scored 1710 runs in eleven test matches, at an average of 90.00. It was a world record for 30 years until Mohammad Yousuf of Pakistan broke it in 2006. T20 cricket didn't exist when Sir Viv was playing. But if it had, he would have been a T20 superstar as well as a test match and one—day giant.

He knew all about Sir Viv's greatness. He'd spent hours watching videos of him batting, and had spent the same length of time listening to interviews in which he unlocked the secrets of the game.

'Come with me, please. We can go to my office. Well, it's not really my office. It's an empty office that I'm allowed to use, to do my studying.

'I'm preparing for university, you see. To study economics. Money and business, and supply and demand. All that sort of stuff. It'll help me. Later on, I mean. When I get a chance to work for my uncle full-time …'

Viv led the way through a maze of corridors and up a flight of stairs.

He was a little above medium height, with long legs. As he walked, he bounced off the balls of his feet, like he was running in to bowl.

His hair was dark and messy. He wore a blue suit, and a white shirt without a tie.

As they went, Frank saw more pictures on the walls, as well as a display-cabinet filled with bats of different shapes and sizes.

He could hear the sounds of the factory echoing around the building.

Whoomps and whooshes.

Clanks and jangles.

Thuds and clunks.

He even thought he could hear the familiar sound of a bowling machine somewhere close by.

'Would you like a sneak peek at the factory floor?' asked Viv, turning round as he reached the top of the stairs.

'Sounds good', said Frank.

'We'll go this way, then', said Viv, pointing left.

They passed along another corridor. On one side, there was a sequence of doors, labelled with job titles Frank had no idea existed:

'Bat Whisperer.'

'Handle Crafter.'

'Edge Sculptor.'

'Density Chemist.'

'Balance Master.'

The other side was exposed brick, painted white, until about half-way down. Then a wide rectangular window took over.

Viv stopped, smiled at Frank, and pointed towards the glass.

It was like nothing he had ever seen before.

Down below, on the factory floor, dozens of men and women were working in harmony with a host of remarkable-looking machines.

There were machines that were almost certainly spaceships.

Machines resembling shrunken windmills.

Machines that looked like gigantic, robotic spiders.

One reminded Frank of an ice-cream cone he'd once had, where the ice-cream man had balanced three scoops on top of one another, and then stuck two flakes in the top.

He let out a low whistle, smiled, and shook his head.

'You should see the factory in West Bengal', said Viv, laughing. 'That makes this one look like a playground.'

He gave Frank a minute to take it all in.

'What's that one for?' Frank asked, pressing his finger up against the glass.

'That's the Automated Tarantula Knocker-Inner. My uncle designed the original. You're looking at version 16.'

'It knocks in bats automatically, so you don't have to. There's a cricket ball attached to each leg. They line up eight bats underneath, then it starts to rotate, and each leg knocks in each bat in turn.

'It's a great time-saver.'

Viv set off down the corridor.

'Not far now: we're nearly there.'

Frank had to tear himself away from the window.

He could have spent all day standing next to the glass, watching the people and the machines working in unison.

By the time he looked up, Viv had disappeared round a corner.

He skipped along the corridor and caught up with him.

'Ta-da!' Viv said, throwing open an oak door.

'My office.'

He winked and gestured with his thumb.

'The headquarters!'

Frank followed him inside.

'It's small, but I'm only starting out.'

Viv grabbed hold of his desk and yanked it away from the wall.

'Pull up a pew', he said, pointing to a green swivel chair in the corner. 'I've got something to show you.'

Moving the table meant that there was enough space for Frank to wheel the chair across and slide it in beside Viv, who was busy logging onto his computer.

'Real live footage', he said, his voice rising with excitement.

'Of who?' asked Frank, his mind still catching up after the marvellous machines of the factory floor.

'Of The Stump Smasher, of course! The first member of our team.'

'Mr Chatterjee filled you in on everything then?'

Viv laughed.

'Mr Chatterjee … it's funny hearing you call him that. Most people here call him D.K. I just call him 'Uncle'.

'He told me about last night. About Jago Lillywhite Grace. And', he lowered his voice, 'The League of the Stuffed Shirts.'

'He also told me about what you did, Frank. It was brave.'

'I've been waiting all morning to meet you. I think we're going to get along well.'

Frank was beginning to think so too.

'Do you play?' asked Frank. 'Cricket, I mean.'

'Is a green-top good for fast bowlers?'

Frank laughed.

'So that's a 'yes', then?'

Viv nodded.

'I'm a fast bowler. Or I try to be, anyway. But this guy makes me look like a tortoise carrying a sack of potatoes on my back.'

He pointed at the laptop. A video was loaded up. Viv clicked 'play'.

Frank watched as a teenage boy appeared on screen, wearing cricket whites.

He was tall. At least six foot tall. And he looked like he still had room to grow.

On each wrist he had a sweatband. One green, the other orange. And he was wearing a headband, a sheaf of blonde hair flopping over the thick band of white fabric.

The camera followed the boy as he marked out his run-up.

He turned and faced the wicket.

Someone threw him the ball.

It was shiny on one side, dull on the other.

He caught it, twirled it in his fingers a couple of times, brought his hands together, stretched them out in front, and started to run.

It was like watching a tiger sprinting after its prey.

He bounded to the crease, knees pumping, hair bouncing up and down over the top of his headband.

Nearing the umpire, his strides shortened, his left arm shot out.

He leapt, drove forwards.

In a single, sweeping motion, his right arm whirled round.

Hitting the ground, he shouted. Loud, guttural, indecipherable.

As the ball left his hand, his whole body strained, every ounce of energy channelled up his arm, into his fingers and injected into the ball.

It flew from his grip, like a dark red cannonball fired from a castle's battlements.

He carried on moving, stumbling in his follow-through, the power and speed of his own bowling sending him tumbling.

The batter played a cover drive.

Only, by the time he got round to playing it, his bails were flying through the air and his stumps were splayed across the ground.

Whoops of delight erupted from the computer's speakers. The wicketkeeper clapped his heavy blue gloves together, and roared.

The bowler sprang from the floor, leapt into the air, and pumped his fists.

For a second, the batter held his pose, then looked behind, and shook his head.

Frank smiled. He'd been there himself. You had to feel some sympathy for the guy.

Viv paused the video and turned to Frank.

'What do you think?' he asked.

'Rapid', said Frank, raising his eyebrows. 'Very rapid. What's his name?'

'Connor Knight. He plays for Accrington Academicals in the Lancashire leagues. They have a game tonight, against Digglebeck Cricket Club.'

Frank felt a jolt of excitement in the pit of his stomach. Nervous energy, the same as when he was at the crease, waiting to face a bowler like this Connor Knight.

Although few he had faced were as fast as this boy looked.

'Perfect', said Frank. 'How do we get there?'

Viv smiled.

'Already sorted, my friend. I'll drive us.'

Chapter Fifteen:
A Shadowy Shape

iv had a car. A small purple hatchback with a pair of bails tied together on a short piece of string, and hung behind the rear-view mirror.

It turned out he was four months older than Frank.

They had a lot in common, starting with their love of cricket.

Through the afternoon, they got to know each other.

Viv showed Frank around. Unfortunately, the factory floor was out of bounds.

You needed a special pass to get down there. And it took a day for anyone to be approved.

It was about security. There were lots of people out there who wanted to steal the secrets of Chatterjee's Bats.

But Viv insisted that Frank should tell him when he was next in Manchester. That way, he could get him a pass and show him the machines up close.

They had lunch late in the day.

The two of them left the factory and walked back into the Manchester city centre.

Viv knew a place called Paradise Pizza that served pizza by the slice.

The owner made sure that there were always a dozen flavours on the go.

Frank was hungry.

He helped himself to five of them: double pepperoni explosion, goat's cheese garden supreme, mama's original margherita, barbecue smokestack surprise, and cheesy veggie meltdown.

They finished things off with a slice of dessert pizza. Something he'd never tried before.

Lemon curd, icing sugar, and basil leaves came together in a taste explosion.

It was delicious.

They talked about The League of the Stuffed Shirts, and the terrible plans Jago had in store for the world of cricket.

Viv shook his head in disgust.

Then he listened in rapt attention as Frank detailed what had happened at The Ancient Assembly of Cricket.

Both the secret meeting he'd unexpectedly become a part of, and the events of the gala dinner.

Hearing it first-hand made it feel more real to Viv than when his uncle had told him over the phone.

Finally, Frank explained about Dorian, and how Jago's loyal underling had followed him to Manchester.

When he told Viv about this, they both couldn't help but look over their shoulders, scanning the restaurant for any signs that they were being watched.

If they were, it wasn't by Dorian. But who knew who else was working for The League of the Stuffed Shirts?

It wasn't long before the factory whistle sounded, signalling the end of the shift.

The evening workers trooped onto the factory floor, talking and joking as they went.

The factory ran for sixteen hours a day. It had to. It was hard work making enough bats to keep the cricketers of England, Wales, Scotland, and Northern Ireland supplied.

'Time for us to go', said Viv. 'Are you ready?'

Frank nodded. 'Let's hope this Connor Knight likes what we have to say.'

Between the two of them, they had spent over an hour planning how they were going to explain the situation to The Stump Smasher. What they would say — but, also, what they would leave out.

It was a fine balance.

They didn't want to spread too much information about The League of the Stuffed Shirts. And no one could know about the bet between Jago and Mr Chatterjee.

There were some things they could say, though. First, that an important match was going to be played at The Ancient Assembly of Cricket. And second, that the owner of Chatterjee's Bats would like to invite Mr Connor Knight to play for his team.

That might be enough to persuade him.

They were soon heading north on the motorway, towards Accrington.

Viv's car talked to them as they drove, grunting and groaning, whirring and clicking. It sounded to Frank like the whole thing was crying out for a trip to the garage.

'Sorry about the noises', said Viv. 'They came with the car.'

Frank laughed.

He was excited. The Stump Smasher was exactly the kind of player they needed to open the bowling.

All they had to do was convince him to sign up, then they could fill the first space on their team sheet.

That, and avoid Dorian or any other members of The League who might try and upset their plans.

'We need a name', said Viv. 'For the team. The D.K. Chatterjee Invitational Eleven is a bit of a mouthful.

'Do you know what Jago's going to call his team?'

'No', said Frank. 'But it wouldn't surprise me if he calls them 'The Privileged Few', or 'Jago's Elite Aristocrats'.'

Now it was Viv's turn to laugh.

Frank joined in, smiling and chuckling.

'We need something modern', he said. 'Something that grabs people's attention. Like Sunrisers Hyderabad or Perth Scorchers.'

'Trinbago Knight Riders', said Viv. 'That's a good one.'*

They went quiet for a bit, both trying to think of a name that sounded right.

---

* Sunrisers Hyderabad play in the Indian Premier League (IPL). Perth Scorchers play in the Big Bash League (BBL), in Australia. And Trinbago Knight Riders play in the Caribbean Premier League (CPL).

In the background, the radio was playing.

The road was busy. It was the end of the day. Lots of people had finished work in Manchester, and were heading home. The surrounding countryside was dotted with villages and towns.

Frank noticed that Viv kept looking in his rear-view mirror. More than was necessary.

'Everything OK?' he asked.

'I'm not sure', said Viv. 'I think someone might be following us.'

Thoughts of what to name their team faded away.

Frank levered himself round, gripped hold of his seat and looked out of the rear window.

There were dozens of cars behind them, as well as lorries, a coach, and a couple of motorbikes.

'Which one do you think it is?'

Viv checked his mirror again.

'The silver Mercedes. I've been seeing it ever since we left the factory. And it always seems to be the same distance behind us. Like it's keeping us in its sights.'

Frank tried to get a better look.

It was too far away. The driver was a shadowy shape in the car.

'Do you think it's Dorian?' asked Viv.

Frank returned to his normal position in the passenger seat.

'It could be. Or it could be someone else working for The League of the Stuffed Shirts.'

'If it's Dorian, how did he find us?' asked Viv.

'Maybe he was waiting outside the factory, keeping watch.'

'Do you think he's following us to see where we go?'

'It wouldn't surprise me. I think The League of the Stuffed Shirts will try anything to stop us winning.'

'If they can get to the players we want before us, they might prevent us from putting a team together'

'Then we'd lose automatically. Without even having a chance to play the game.'

Viv scowled.

'They are the worst', he said. 'What about the spirit of cricket? What about playing the game the right way?'

Frank was looking in the wing mirror, trying to see if he could make out the driver of the silver Mercedes.

'They don't think like that', he said. 'Jago only cares about himself and getting his hands on power. To him, the rules don't matter. He'll do anything to get what he wants. We need to be careful.'

137

Viv kept his eyes on the road. A sign indicated that the next turn-off was for Accrington.

'We're going to put together the best team in the world', he said, the heat of anger in his voice. 'And we'll show Jago and all his lackeys what cricket is really about.'

Frank gave up squinting into the wing mirror and started to laugh.

'What?' asked Viv, wondering what his friend thought was so funny.

'Nothing', said Frank. 'I was just remembering what Dorian was wearing when I saw him. A big brown double-breasted overcoat, sunglasses, and a tweed cap. He looked like he fell into a costume box and climbed out dressed as the world's worst spy.'

Viv started laughing.

'If he is following us, I think he'll be easy to spot when we get there!'

It felt good to lighten the mood.

And it wasn't long before they were pulling into the car-park of the Accrington Academicals, five minutes before the match was due to start.

Chapter Sixteen:
Dorian Makes a Play

he Accrington Academicals cricket ground was at the end of an untarred road, on the far side of town.

The clubhouse looked at least a hundred years old, and was made of wood and peeling paint. Next to it was a more modern brick building, housing the changing rooms, showers, players' lockers, and a general-purpose meeting room.

The pitch was not quite an oval — more a squashed circle, with a chunk bitten out of the bottom where an enormous oak tree towered over the boundary edge.

An old-fashioned scoreboard sat beyond the clubhouse, on a 45-degree angle to the wicket.

To enter, the scorer had to climb a rickety ladder, open a trap-door, and squeeze through a hole designed for someone a little bit smaller.

Both teams were milling around on the outfield.

As Viv and Frank got out of the car, they saw the two captains come together for the coin toss.

Accrington won, and chose to bat.

'Looks like we'll have to wait to see him bowl', said Viv.

'Maybe we can chat to him while they're batting. He'll probably be coming in down the order.'

'Sounds like a plan', said Viv, as he locked the car. 'Any sign of the Mercedes?'

Frank looked around.

The car-park was full. They had grabbed the last space.

'No', he said, slowly. 'I can't see it. But let's keep our eyes open. We might not be the only ones here.'

They walked across the tarmac, and past a couple of benches set into the grass near the boundary.

Digglebeck's fielders were spreading themselves out round the pitch. A fast bowler with a shaved head was stretching near the end of his run-up.

The Digglebeck captain was talking to him and making gestures with his hands, showing the fielders where they should go. The fast bowler tossed the ball into the air and caught it. Once, twice, three times.

From the clubhouse came the umpires, wearing white coats and broad-brimmed hats.

Close behind them were Accrington's opening batters.

One was small and squat, and had an enormous belly. The other was tall and gangly. They looked like two halves of an unlikely pair. Both helmeted, both swinging their bats.

'Let's watch a couple of overs', said Viv. 'Then we'll go and find him.'

'OK', said Frank, and the two of them took up position on one of the benches between the clubhouse and the car-park.

The first over was an uneven affair. The skinhead fast bowler raced up to the crease and sent down a barrage of short balls.

His accuracy wasn't good. The gangly opener was able to cut two wide balls away for four.

Frank and Viv watched as they changed ends. Neither spoke. A tension had arisen. They both knew the time was coming when they would have to try and persuade The Stump Smasher to join them. And what if he said no?

The next over was bowled by a medium pacer, who was much slower, and much more accurate.

The opener with the enormous belly swung wildly at every ball that came down.

He missed the first five, the last of which passed within a fingernail of off stump.

And on the sixth ball, he connected.

It sounded like a heavy wooden door being slammed shut.

The ball rocketed off the middle of his bat, straight back over the bowler's head.

It flew into the sky, sailing in a perfect arc until it landed in a field next to the pitch, a good fifteen metres beyond the boundary.

'Shot!' someone shouted.

A few of the fielders shook their heads. The wicketkeeper clapped his hands together, while the bowler put his hands on his hips and delivered a double teapot.[*]

Frank looked at Viv and raised his eyebrows.

'He can sure hit them', he said.

'That's all he ever does', said someone nearby. 'Swing, swing, swing. I've never seen him run a single. Or run at all, for that matter.'

Viv and Frank looked at the huge belly of the batter out in the middle. It hung over the top of his trousers like foam hanging over the side of a bath.

---

[*] The 'double teapot' is a special stance reserved for bowlers, and sometimes for fielders. It involves the player placing one hand on each hip and jutting out their elbows. This makes them look like a teapot with two handles. It is often a signal that the player can't quite believe what has just happened, and believes that the cricketing gods are singling them out for punishment, above everybody else. In wider life, the 'double teapot' is a special invention of the eccentric English tea connoisseur, Sir Rumbelow Scarcroft, who used it to pour two cups of tea at the same time, one to drink, and one to pour on his pot-plants.

'Excuse me', asked Viv. 'You don't happen to know Connor Knight, do you? We were hoping to talk to him.'

The man he had spoken to was dressed in a dark blue tracksuit. He had a face that made him look older than he was, covered in creases, and with a bristly moustache.

'That's funny', he said, walking the short distance to where Viv and Frank were sitting. 'You're the second person who's asked to speak to Connor. Word must be getting around about the Stump Smasher.'

The stranger scratched his ear and smiled.

'Phil's the name. Phil Butterworth.'

'I coach Connor. Not that he needs much from me. Not like some of the other lads. What do you want to speak to him about?'

'Someone else is here?' asked Frank, looking round.

He was alert, his eyes checking the area, searching for Dorian or any sign that The League of the Stuffed Shirts were in attendance.

'That's right. Another lad arrived a few minutes before. Young, like you two. Said he had an offer to make. To Connor, like. Wanted him to play in a special match at The Ancient Assembly of Cricket.'

'What an honour that would be.'

'One of our lads down in London, representing the Academicals.'

'We'd be thrilled if he got picked. Absolutely thrilled. Connor's a super lad. Very fast. Very hard working. And Accrington could do with a bit of recognition on the big stage. Long time coming, if you ask me.'

Viv and Frank listened closely, trying not to show any emotion.

'When we lost the toss, I sent the two of them off to have a chat. Connor's a great bowler. Probably the best I've ever coached at his age. Not much of a batter, mind. They never are though, are they? Fast bowlers. Don't usually like getting the pads on. They know what real pace is. And they have the good sense to steer clear of it.'

Phil laughed. It was a friendly laugh. A laugh that saw the fun in life.

'Unless we have a complete collapse, I don't think we'll need him till the change of innings.'

Frank and Viv had lost all interest in the match.

They were both standing up, trying not to look suspicious, but struggling to contain their concern. Dorian was here. And he'd beaten them to the ground.

What would The Stump Smasher do?

If he signed for Jago's team, it would be a disaster.

Not only would they lose out on their first-choice fast bowler, but they'd also have to face off against him as well.

'Um, can you remember the name of the chap?' asked Frank, working hard to make his voice sound normal.

'Friend of yours, is he?'

'Could be. We came in separate cars.'

'You two are here about the match as well, then?'

Viv stepped forward and thrust out his hand.

'V.I.V. Chatterjee', he said, 'Chatterjee's Bats. Call me Viv. Yes, we're here about the match. We would like Connor to play for the D.K. Chatterjee Invitational Eleven.'

Phil smiled.

Frank appreciated Viv's quick thinking.

Bringing Chatterjee's Bats into the equation was surely going to be a good move.

'That name's a bit of a mouthful isn't it?'

The coach chuckled and rubbed his chin.

'Chatterjee's Bats, eh? Pleased to meet you Viv. I've been using the Blastmaster 2000 for the last eight years. It's a brilliant bat.'

He turned to Frank and held out a hand, waiting for him to introduce himself.

'Er, I'm Frank. Frank Meadows …'

Frank shook Phil's hand and glanced at Viv.

'Associate of Chatterjee's Bats', said Viv, quickly. 'Junior Batting Consultant. Apprentice Handle Crafter.'

'Impressive', said Phil. 'You'll have to give me some tips, Frank.'

Frank opened his mouth but didn't know what to say.

Viv spoke instead.

'Could we have a word with Connor, sir. If that's not too much trouble?'

A cheer went up as the big-bellied opening batter slapped a huge six over extra cover. Phil turned away from the conversation, to watch the game.

'Sure, lads. Sure. I think they went round the back of the scorer's box. To the nets. Connor probably wanted to show what he could do, seeing as how we're batting first.'

'Great — thanks Phil', said Viv.

'Any time you want to upgrade your Blastmaster, come down to Manchester and ask for me. I'll personally see to it that you get the best service possible.'

Phil turned away from the match and gave Viv a thoughtful look.

'That sounds like a great offer, Viv. Thank you. I might just have to take you up on that.'

The Accrington Academicals coach pointed towards the middle of the pitch.

'We could be in for fireworks, today', he said. 'It looks like Big Dunc's in the zone.'

The coach was keen to finish the conversation. He didn't want to miss any more play.

'Just one question, Phil', said Frank, 'if you don't mind. Did the other lad give you a name?'

'What's that?' asked Phil, who whistled as a slow leg cutter turned past the edge of Big Dunc's bat.

'A name? Yes … Florian, I think. No, wait. Dorian, that was it. Got some size on him. Seemed nice enough.'

'I thought you said he was with you?'

He turned to look at them as he asked the question.

But there was no one there.

Frank and Viv were running round the boundary edge, haring towards the gap between the clubhouse and the scorer's box.

Chapter Seventeen:
The Stump Smasher

et back from the clubhouse were three nets, in a row. Emerald-green netting hung from black steel poles. Two of the nets had artificial wickets laid. The third was grass, cut as short as it would go.

Around the nets the grass was long and bushy, dotted with dandelions and daisies.

The noises of the match were quieter here, dampened by the buildings and the distance.

Frank saw him first.

He was standing at the end of the furthest net, the one with the grass, next to a single stump wedged into the ground.

The overcoat was gone.

So were the tweed cap and sunglasses.

He was wearing an expensive-looking suit, a pale blue shirt, and a silver tie.

Dressed like that, there was less to laugh about.

And more to fear.

He looked respectable.

Presentable.

Believable.

They might be too late.

Dorian saw them as they slowed to a trot.

He smiled.

It was an arrogant smile. The smile of someone who thinks they've won without trying.

The smile of a person who takes great pleasure rubbing everyone else's faces in it.

As Frank and Viv neared him, their pace now slow and uncertain, a whirlwind stormed into view.

It sprinted into the gap between them and Dorian, leapt off the ground, and crashed down beside the stump.

A blur of white and blonde, orange and green.

A spherical red rocket exploded out of The Stump Smasher's hand. It was like a missile bombing through the air. Tearing towards its target. Setting new records for the immensity of its speed.

There was a thumping clatter as the ball collided with middle stump.

'Bravo! Bravo!'* called Dorian clapping his hands together. 'Mr Grace will be impressed.'

---

* Not to be confused with the West Indian all-rounder Dwayne Bravo, a fantastic player who is the first person ever to take 500 wickets in T20 cricket. He has played for many great teams around the world, including Chennai Super Kings, Peshawar Zalmi, Melbourne Stars, and Trinbago

The Stump Smasher regained his balance, took a breath, and marched down the net. First he retrieved the ball. Then he reset the stumps. The ball was his. And he never let any batter forget it.

Knight Riders. He helped West Indies win both the 2012 and 2016 Twenty20 World Cups.

Dorian flashed a quick look at Frank and Viv.

'Too late', he hissed. 'Losers don't win.'

Frank ignored him and watched The Stump Smasher walk back up the wicket towards them.

He was wearing his distinctive sweatbands. One on each wrist, and one on his head. Green, orange, and white.

His wavy blonde hair flopped over his headband, just like in the video. Each of his eyes was a different colour. One blue, one brown. A band of freckles ran across his cheeks and nose.

'All right', he said. 'Are you guys here for the demo as well?'

'Those are the colours of the Indian flag', said Viv, pointing at Connor's sweat bands.

'And the Irish', he replied. 'That's where my mammy's from.'

He shined one side of the ball on his trousers.

'I'll do an off cutter for you this time. It's a little slower, but you don't want to bowl every ball the same, do you? Need to get the batter guessing. Need to get into his head.'

The three of them watched as The Stump Smasher walked back to his mark, steamed in, and sent another red torpedo towards the wickets.

This one came out a touch slower, but not by much. It hit the deck and moved, subtly, in towards the stumps. Just enough to make life even harder for a batter.

Again, there was the sound of the ball hitting wood and the sight of bails flying into the air.

Connor Knight turned round and beamed back down the track. He held his hands in the air, pointing his index fingers to the sky.

'Another one bites the dust!', he said. 'Does Mr Grace know what a great bowler he's signed up?'

The Stump Smasher was big for his age, with broad shoulders and a strong chest. He had a lot of power to call on, and his bowling action ensured that every ounce of it ended up in the ball.

'Connor', he said, stretching his hand towards Frank and Viv. 'Are you guys with Dorian?'

They shook hands and introduced themselves.

'Chatterjee's Bats? Wow, that's cool. I try to bowl fast enough so the lad at the other end hasn't got time to use his bat. Even if it is a Chatterjee!'

There was the hint of an Irish accent in his voice.

The conversation died and the four of them stood there.

An awkward moment went by.

Dorian broke the silence:

'Meadows and his chum aren't with me, Connor. Mr Grace is very careful when deciding who he works with. Very careful. These two …' Dorian flicked his hand at Frank and Viv, like he was trying to waft away a bad smell. 'They don't meet the standards Mr Grace likes to keep. Don't come close.'

Connor raised an eyebrow.

In the background, a great shout went up.

'That's either another six, or Dunc's been bowled through the gate.'*

The awkward silence returned.

'So … do you two want to tell me what you're doing here? I mean … if you're not working for Mr Grace, who are you working for?'

Dorian listened with amusement as Frank and Viv made their pitch to Connor.

---

* 'The gate' is the gap between the bat and the pad. The gate often appears when a batter doesn't move his feet. He swings at the ball, or prods the bat out, and the gate appears. If the bowler can get the ball to move, he can send it through the gate and have a chance of hitting the wickets.

They trod carefully, avoiding all mention of The League of the Stuffed Shirts, the wager made between D.K. and Jago, and the contents of the contract.

Dorian enjoyed seeing the two of them struggling to put their case. They were flustered. Still trying to get their heads around the fact that Jago's henchman had beaten them to the club.

He took pleasure at watching them toil, as they tried to explain to Connor why he should play for them, instead of for Jago's team.

How he would have loved to burst out laughing and jab a finger in their faces. He wanted to taunt them. Wanted to remind them that his boss was not only the newly elected Governor of OINC, but also the head of The League of the Stuffed Shirts.

But most of all, he wanted to tell them that they should give up now, because there was no way they would win the match.

It was hopeless. The League was too powerful. It had massive resources. And Dorian was only one of hundreds, if not thousands, whom it could call on to do its work.

As Frank and Viv came to the end of their pitch, he decided he would drive the rented Mercedes all the way back to London and drop it off down there.

It would be quicker than waiting for a train.

And he would have fewer northerners to deal with

He didn't like the north. Manchester smelt funny, and Accrington was about as interesting as a documentary on the history of tractors.

The sooner he could get out of there, the better. All he needed was Connor's signature on a contract, and he was done.

'Impressive pitch', said Connor.

'Thanks', said Frank, a sense of relief washing over him.

'It puts a different spin on things.'

Dorian's eyes had glazed over as he daydreamed about returning to London.

Now he was alert.

'What?' he hissed, a certain roughness in his voice. 'We have a deal, Knight. You agreed it.'

Connor tossed the ball into the air and caught it, one-handed.

'We *had* a deal', he said. 'But that was before I knew there was another offer. You have to look after yourself in this business.'

'I couldn't agree more', said Viv, putting his arm round Connor's shoulder. 'Did I mention that we can arrange an exclusive tour of the Chatterjee bat factory if you sign for us?'

'Interesting', said Connor. 'I bet coach would like that as well.'

'He can come', said Viv, sensing an opportunity. 'In fact, you can bring the whole team. A special behind-the-scenes tour for Accrington Academicals. Plus, a free prototype Blastmaster 3000 for every player. You can help us with our testing.'

'Hang on', said Dorian, jabbing his finger like he was hammering away at a button that didn't work. 'We have a deal. We agreed it. These two are a pair of muppets! They don't know what they're –'

Connor shrugged off Viv's arm, spun round and put a firm hand on Dorian's shoulder.

'No need for rudeness, Mr Dorian. We haven't signed anything yet. I'm free to negotiate with whoever I want.'

Dorian spluttered.

'Mr Grace has made you an offer, Knight. You'd do well to accept it.'

'Mr Knight is free to make his own decisions', said Viv. 'I'm sure he can weigh up both offers. He doesn't need you telling him what to think.'

Connor threw the ball in the air again and caught it.

'Listen, guys. It's flattering. Really it is. This match you lot have got planned sounds great. And I'd love to be involved.'

'You've made good offers. The way I see it, there isn't much between them.'

Dorian snorted, indicating his disagreement.

'So, how about this. You both get padded up and I'll fire down an over at each of you. Whoever plays me better, they get my signature.'

It wasn't what any of them had been expecting. Least of all Dorian.

Jago's henchman bit his lip, pointed his finger and was on the verge of unleashing a tirade of abuse before he stopped himself and forced a smarmy, false smile across his face. The image of a furious Jago had floated across his mind, reminding him what was waiting back in London if he failed.

'You'll have to choose who pads up', said Connor, gesturing at Frank and Viv. 'But you, Dorian, you're the only one who can represent Mr Grace.'

'So, you'll have to bat.'

Dorian tried to control his face. He tried to keep the fake smile intact. He tried to hide the panic rising inside him at the thought of facing six balls from the Stump Smasher.

But he couldn't control the beetroot-coloured flush spreading across his cheeks.

As for Frank, he knew it would be him who would face The Stump Smasher.

He was the batter.

Viv was the bowler.

It would be tough.

Really tough.

But what a challenge it was. What an opportunity!

Viv slapped him on the back.

'Frank will go for us. I'm a bowler.'

Dorian's eyes narrowed to a pair of small slits.

He was not a batter.

He did not like batting.

Not one bit.

He hated it.

And he especially did not like batting against searing-hot lightning-fast pace.

But the thought of disappointing Jago was worse than the thought of facing six balls from Connor.

'Fine', he said, through clenched teeth, his cheeks and forehead covered in a deep red blush. 'Let's do it. Mr Grace will be delighted to know you turned his offer into a party game. Delighted.'

Connor thrust his arm into the air, the ball in his hand.

'Game on!' he said. 'I'll go easy on you. For the first three balls, anyway.'

He laughed.

'We've got some spare kit in the clubhouse, follow me.'

'And I've got a few bats in the boot of the car', said Viv. 'Chatterjee specials.'

'Excellent', said Connor.

As they walked off together, Dorian skulked at the back, grumbling under his breath, and cursing the day he had ever set foot in Accrington.

Chapter Eighteen: Six Balls from The Stump Smasher

orian shouted 'heads', as Connor tossed a coin into the air.

It was heads.

'I'll go first', he said. 'Show you how it's done.'

Viv and Frank stood to the side. They were well positioned to watch Connor run in. And the angle meant they also had a good view of Dorian.

Slouching, dragging his bat behind him, he reached the stumps.

'Jago had better appreciate this', he thought.

Deep down, though, he knew Jago didn't appreciate anything other than himself.

He turned and asked for a guard.

Viv skipped over to the single stump.

'Middle', barked Dorian, holding his bat away from him, in line with the stumps.

'A little that way', said Viv, making a shuffling movement with his hand.

'That's middle.'

Dorian scraped a mark into the ground and shooed Viv away.

'Charming', he said to Frank, as he got back into position.

Frank didn't say anything. He was concentrating. Trying to relax.

He'd faced fast bowling before.

The first thing was not to fear it.

The second thing was to block out what was happening around you.

The third thing was to focus, to watch the ball, and to get your bat up nice and high, in position. Ready to play.

Connor stuck his left arm in the air and gave a thumbs up.

Dorian adjusted his helmet, checked his pads, his gloves, and his chest guard.

'Let's go!', he shouted.

Then, under his breath: 'and get this over with.'

Connor started his run up.

Frank followed with his eyes, staring not at The Stump Smasher, but at the ball.

He watched as it reached the crease.

Watched as it rose upwards.

Watched as it left Connor's hand.

Watched as it sailed through the air, hit the pitch, bounced, then zoomed past Dorian at shoulder height.

Viv let out a whistle.

'He. Is. Fast. Faster than me by a long way. He's like a whirlwind. I'd love to get a speed-gun on him and see what he clocks in at.'

Frank broke his concentration.

'Thanks, Viv', he said. 'Maybe save all that until after I've faced him.'

The next two balls were identical to the first. Fast. Accurate. Short. But not too short.

And Dorian didn't get his bat near either of them.

It looked to Frank and Viv like he was inching towards the leg side. Trying to put more distance between himself and the balls Connor was bowling.

It was as if he didn't want to be there.

Really didn't want to be there.

Like he wanted to be somewhere else, many miles away, where The Stump Smasher was only a distant memory.

Not that they blamed him.

Connor was an intimidating bowler.

Difficult to face.

Hard to defend against.

Even harder to score off.

But it was interesting to see Dorian not quite living up to the image he projected.

'Right, you've had some sighters. Now I'll give you something to hit', shouted Connor, as he turned at the top of his run and began to race back towards the crease.

He flew past Viv and Frank, sprang into the air, crashed to earth, and let fly a thunderbolt.

Dorian closed his eyes, lurched to the side, and swung his bat.

The ball clattered into the stumps, flattening all three.

'And he bowls him!' yelled Connor.

It took a couple of minutes to get the stumps back in position.

Dorian looked like a guilty man waiting to be sentenced.

He removed his gloves, put them back on. Fumbled with his pads. Laid his bat on the ground, checked his chest guard. Adjusted his helmet. Picked up his bat and examined the edges. Tapped the middle with a gloved fist.

Anything to delay the agony.

Connor set off again.

White and blonde and orange and green. Racing to the stumps.

It was a carbon-copy of the previous delivery.

Dorian flailed wildly.

His bottom hand left the bat completely.

There was the sound of leather smashing into wood as the stumps were splattered by the full, in-swinging yorker.

'Two out of two!' Connor shouted.

It was obvious to Viv and Frank that he loved taking wickets, even if it was only practice.

'One to go', he said, his voice still excited. 'Are you ready, Frank? Think you can do better than Dorian?'

He winked as he walked past, in the direction of his mark.

Frank picked up his helmet, put it over his head and secured it, in preparation. He was ready. He would do his best.

He would find a way.

Through sheer luck, Dorian managed to connect with Connor's last delivery.

A satisfying noise boomed from the Chatterjee bat, and the ball flew into the netting.

'Four', said Dorian, pointing the bat in the direction of the ball. 'Four all day long.'

He couldn't get out of the net quickly enough.

He half-jogged, half-ran past Connor, who was fetching the ball from where it had ended up.

Dorian stood in front of Frank and Viv while he took his helmet off.

'Beat that', he said, nostrils flaring, beads of sweat trickling down his forehead. 'You haven't got a chance. This lad's signing for Jago. And there's nothing you or your stupid bat can do about it.'

'You're up next, Frank', said Connor, cheerfully.

'Same as Dorian, six balls. I'll go easy on the first three, then I'll give you the tough stuff. Let's see what you've got.'

Frank was in the net, standing beside the stumps.

'Middle and leg, please, Viv', he said.

'That way a bit … a bit more … that's it. Good luck.'

Frank gave a thumbs up, straining the material of his batting glove.

Viv moved to the side. Dorian was standing opposite, unfastening the chest guard he had been wearing on top of his shirt and tie.

'This is it', thought Frank.

Six balls.

An over. Nothing more. Nothing less.

Six balls to secure the signature of The Stump Smasher. One of the brightest young fast bowlers in the land.

All he had to do was bat.

All he had to do was go one better than Dorian.

He'd faced his six balls.

Three dots, bowled twice, and a solitary boundary.

That's what Frank had to beat.

And if he did it, Connor would play for them. For him, D.K., and Viv. For the future of cricket.

And not for Jago.

Frank stepped away from the crease.

He adjusted his helmet. Checked his gloves.

'Get on with it', shouted Dorian. But Frank ignored him.

He jabbed his bat against the floor a couple of times, then twirled it in his hand.

He let his mind empty.

He let the thoughts of what might happen drift away, like mist disappearing in the sunshine.

He wanted clarity. Concentration. Focus.

Frank looked straight ahead. Not at Connor. But at the ball.

He watched it bob and weave as Connor started to run in.

He watched it rise up as Connor hit the crease and leapt into the air.

He watched it come towards him at tremendous speed as Connor propelled it forwards with all his power.

Short, back of a length.

Outside off stump.

He watched it all the way as it whizzed past him.

Watched it as it thumped into the padding that lined the back of the net.

And he continued to watch it as he walked towards it. Even though it wasn't moving any more.

He watched it as he bent down and picked it up.

And he kept watching it as Connor caught it and walked the long walk to the top of his mark.

The next ball was similar but wider.

It left Connor's hand, tore through the air like a meteor piercing the atmosphere, bounced, reared up, and slammed into the back of the net.

All in barely a second.

Frank's eyes stuck to the ball like glue. He wouldn't let himself look at anything else. It consumed his vision.

All he had to do was watch it.

And keep concentrating.

The third ball was the final sighter. Then Connor would go for the stumps. Like he had done with Dorian.

Frank watched the ball as The Stump Smasher ran in.

It was slightly fuller.

He watched it bounce.

He stepped across his stumps with his back foot. A quick, sharp movement.

His head was completely still.

He swung.

And he connected.

The ball catapulted into the netting.

A strong tremor of force juddered through the bat and up his arms.

'Shot!' said Connor. 'Best one yet. Call it a boundary.'

Frank felt a thrill of excitement tap-dance down his spine.

This was it, he thought. This was their opportunity. He was level with Dorian. One boundary a piece.

Three balls faced. Two dots, one four.

Three balls to go.

He was halfway there.

Halfway to securing the signature of The Stump Smasher.

He could feel his heart beating faster.

He started imagining what it would be like to face Connor in a match. The cheers he would get from his team-mates in the Abbey Road Young Boys First XI as he punched more boundaries through the off side.

Then he stopped, laid his bat on the ground, and began unfastening his batting gloves.

It was an old trick he'd learned from his Dad.

If you lose concentration, you're giving the bowler a chance to get you out.

If you start thinking about other things, instead of the next ball, you need to be careful.

The trick was to slow things down. Pause the action. Make the bowler wait.

Not for long. But long enough.

Frank took a couple of deep breaths as he removed his batting gloves, shook them out, put them back on, then re-fastened them.

He stopped thinking about his team-mates.

He stopped thinking about people cheering.

He stopped thinking about securing Connor's signature for his and D.K.'s team.

And he started thinking about the next ball.

The Stump Smasher collected the ball and trudged back.

While he could recognise when a batter played a good shot, that didn't mean he had to like it.

'Even-stevens', he said to Dorian, as he passed. 'Not like your boundary, that. He actually meant to hit it.'

Connor chuckled as he finished speaking.

Dorian scowled.

Viv turned away and tried to stifle a laugh.

'Give him the hot stuff', barked Dorian. 'See how he likes that.' He stabbed a finger in Frank's direction. 'Then we'll see who handles it better.'

Sure enough, the next ball was a lump of volcanic rock flung directly at the bottom of Frank's off stump.

It took him by surprise, and he played it late.

Too late.

First, he heard the ball smashing into his stumps.

Then he heard Connor's cry of delight.

And, finally, Dorian shouting in a sarcastic voice: 'Nice try, Meadows. Maybe you should hit the ball next time. What do you think?'

'Unlucky', said Connor, as he fetched the ball. 'You picked up the line. I'll give you that.'

Four balls down.

Two dots, one boundary and one splattering of the stumps.

He had to keep going.

He had to avoid getting bowled.

He had to protect his stumps.

For two more balls.

That was it.

All that he needed to do. The sole thing he had to achieve.

For the fifth ball, The Stump Smasher tried repeating his trademark delivery.

This time, Frank was ready for him.

As Connor approached the crease, Frank made a tiny movement with his feet.

He stepped across a couple of inches, towards his off stump.

Connor sent the ball close to where the previous delivery had gone.

It arrowed through the air. Fast and full and straight.

And Frank defended it.

The ball hit his bat hard. He could feel the jarring energy run through the handle and vibrate across his shoulders and chest.

He looked down.

The ball was at his feet.

Still.

Unmoving.

No longer a torpedo trying to blow up his stumps.

All the energy was gone. Dissipated. Now it was just a ball again, like any other.

He bent down, picked it up and tossed it to Connor, who was walking towards him, adjusting his headband.

'You're a great bowler', Frank said. 'Deadly.'

Connor caught the ball.

'Ta', he replied. 'I do my best. One left. See if I can get you again.'

Frank refastened the Velcro on his gloves.

He went over the score in his head.

Five balls. Three dots. One boundary. One wicket.

Survive this last ball and they'd won.

He checked his pads, walked a little way down the wicket and used his bat to tap the ground.

He was looking for firmness. Making sure there wasn't a risk of uneven bounce.

'Great bowling', said Viv as Connor walked past. 'We could really use someone like you to test the strength of our new range of bats.'

'Pipe down, Chatterjee', said Dorian. 'No interfering.'

Viv held his hands up and made himself look innocent.

'OK, last ball', said Connor. He was at the top of his run, facing down towards the net, his eyes fixed on the stumps, his nostrils scenting the possibility of another wicket.

He felt the ball in his hand, looked down at it and found the seam.

He placed his thumb underneath and his index finger on top. His middle finger gripped the ball on the side.

He was setting up for the off cutter.

As he bowled, he would release his thumb at the last moment. Then he would pull down on the side of the ball so it would spin, grip, and move in towards the stumps.

A great technique for bamboozling a batter who was expecting something else entirely.

He started to move, trotting at first, then jogging, then running, then racing. Each stride quicker than the last.

He swept past Viv and Dorian.

He leapt.

As the ball left his hand it started to turn.

Frank didn't spot the change in Connor's action. All his focus was on the speed of the delivery.

The ball arrowed through the air.

Frank moved towards it.

As it landed, the seam hit the wicket.

The ball gripped.

It started to move in, towards Frank.

He saw it late, tried to adjust.

He felt himself overbalancing. His head was too far across.

His legs were in the wrong position.

His weight wasn't where it should be.

But he was watching the ball.

His eyes were completely fixed on its trajectory.

He jammed the bat down.

Jammed it hard into the ground.

Jammed it like the only thing that mattered was to protect his stumps. To make sure they were saved from the ball's attack.

Jammed it just in time, at the last possible moment.

Jammed it and hoped.

The ball careered into the bat, squirted between Frank's legs, and raced past his leg stump, missing by a whisker.

He lost his footing and stumbled forward.

He threw his bat out in front and used it to steady himself.

He looked up, risking a glance, not quite realising that the lack of a noise, the lack of a celebration, meant he had survived. That the ball had missed the stumps.

Connor was standing halfway down the wicket, hands on hips, with a beaming grin on his face.

'Well played', he said.

'Thought I had you there, with the cutter. You just managed to get a little tickle on it.'

Frank spun round and saw his stumps were intact. The ball was resting in the netting, becalmed.

Connor turned and shouted down the track.

'I guess that means you lose, Dorian. Unlucky, mate. I'm going with Frank and Viv.'

Viv started clapping and cheering.

A smile spread across Frank's face, beneath his helmet, lighting up his features. He could hear an invisible crowd cheering, could sense the importance of the moment.

They had him. The Stump Smasher. The first name on the team sheet, and the kind of opening bowler who could make opening batters cower beneath their duvets.

Dorian picked up the bat Viv had lent him, and threw it in the direction of the clubhouse.

'You'll regret this, Knight. All of you will regret this. Wait until Jago hears about this. Just you wait!'

He stormed off, muttering angrily to himself. Kicking the grass as he went.

Frank removed his helmet, followed by his gloves. He put the one inside the other and reached out with his free hand.

Connor took it in his own, and they shook. Viv came down to join them, rubbing his own hands together in delight.

The first player for the D.K. Chatterjee Invitational Eleven was in place.

And what a player he was!

'Fantastic bowling', Frank said. 'It's an honour to have you on the team.'

Chapter Nineteen:
A Secret is Revealed

A few days had passed.

Frank was back in London, sitting on a sofa in Mr Chatterjee's mansion flat, sipping a cup of sweet tea.

D.K. sat opposite, in an old leather armchair.

Between them, on a small antique coffee table, was a signed contract.

But this was not the contract that tied together the members of The League of the Stuffed Shirts.

Instead, it was the contract Connor Knight had signed, agreeing to play for the D.K. Chatterjee Invitational Eleven.

In amongst the legal jargon, there were a few interesting paragraphs.

One said that Connor, his coach, and his team-mates could have a full day's tour of the Chatterjee bat factory in Manchester, hosted by D.K. himself, at a time of their choosing.

It also said that D.K., Viv, and Frank would take the whole lot of them out afterwards for a slap-up meal at Paradise Pizza, and that special requests for pizza flavours should be made in advance.

Another paragraph said that Chatterjee's Bats (Manchester) Limited would start paying Connor to work there, part-time, in between his cricket and his studies.

His title would be: 'Consulting Bat Strength Tester'.

His main duties were to bowl as fast as he could at a range of bats. This would help the engineers decide if they were strong enough to cope with express pace.

'You've done a fine job, Mr Meadows', said D.K., raising his cup of tea in acknowledgement of Frank's efforts.

'We have the first piece of the jigsaw. It is a good start. But also, only that. A start.

'There are ten more pieces we need to find if we are to have a chance of beating the team Jago Lillywhite Grace intends to put out.'

Frank tried not to think about the cold, hard grip of Number One's fingers wrapped round his wrist.

The grip he had felt in the Larwood Suite only a few days before.

His thoughts were interrupted by a knock at the door.

'Ah-ha', said D.K., 'he's here.'

A moment later, Virender Ishan Vivek Chatterjee, Viv to his friends, and to everybody else as well, was sitting on the sofa next to Frank, a broad smile plastered across his face.

By his feet was a large rucksack.

'The rest of my stuff is in the car, Uncle', he said.

Mr Chatterjee raised an eyebrow.

'Is it, now?' he asked. 'Are you planning on moving in permanently, then?'

Frank smiled.

'I have a lot of kit', said Viv. 'Plus a dozen bats. And my textbooks.'

'Then there's my clothes, computer, other books, radio, desk-lamp, towels, bedding, pictures, posters, newspaper cuttings, desk chair, pinboard, bedside table, and half a dozen tins of baked beans.'

'And you managed to fit all that into your car?' asked D.K.

'Oh yes', said Viv. 'That's why Frank had to take the train. There wasn't much space left.'

Viv had decided to give up his temporary job at the Chatterjee bat factory in Manchester.

Frank had persuaded him to take on a different role.

They had become a duo.

A pair.

A team.

Viv was going to help Frank find the rest of the players they needed for their match against Jago's eleven, in six months' time, at The Ancient Assembly of Cricket.

They were excited. But also apprehensive.

Dorian had left Accrington Academicals in a foul mood. There was no telling what Jago might do next, when he found out that he had been beaten to the signing of The Stump Smasher.

They would need to look out for each other.

The League of the Stuffed Shirts was like an octopus. It had many limbs, stretching away from the centre.

Tentacles spreading through the world of cricket.

All controlled by the brain: the uncaring, calculating brain of Number One.

Dorian was the first opponent he had sent after them.

There was no way he would be the last.

Jago didn't like to lose.

And he didn't like to play by the rules, either.

The next person he sent would be smarter and cleverer than Dorian.

Frank and Viv would have to find a way of getting past whoever it was they were pitted against.

They would have to keep battling The League of the Stuffed Shirts, all the way, until they had the team they needed.

The team the cricketing world needed.

The team that was the only thing standing in the way of Jago's master plan.

And even then, there was still the small matter of winning the match. Who could say what eleven cricketers Jago would put up against them? And who knew what dastardly tricks he might play if things started to go against him?

The game was far from over, but they had got off to a good start.

Now they would have to see what awaited them.

Over the next few hours, Frank helped Viv to empty his car.

The lift was out of service. Two maintenance men in grey overalls were working on the control mechanism.

Together, they carried everything up the many flights of stairs that separated D.K.'s mansion flat from the ground floor.

It was fun.

It felt like the start of an adventure.

They talked about cricket, and about other things.

They relived the six balls Frank had faced from The Stump Smasher. Together, they imagined what it would be like when he opened the bowling for them against Jago's team.

And then they turned their attention to the team's name.

'That reminds me', said Frank, pausing in between floors, a box under his arm. 'We still haven't decided on a name. The D.K. Chatterjee Invitational Eleven is a real mouthful. We need something better.

'Something snappier.

'Something that sticks in people's minds.'

Viv bent down and rested his own box on a step. An economics textbook poked out of the top, along with a biography of Shane Warne.

'Well', he said, 'the whole business seems to have brought out the worst in The League of the Stuffed Shirts.'

'Dorian was pretty unpleasant in Accrington.'

'And I'll bet Jago will be furious with him.'

'So, how about The Stuffed Shirts Stink XI?' Frank cackled.

Viv joined in, guffawing loudly.

The sound of their laughter echoed up the stairwell.

'I'm not sure that's going to work', Frank said, in between giggles.

'No, maybe not', said Viv, wiping a tear from his eye. 'Perhaps we just keep that one to ourselves.'

'What about the Fury Cricket XI?' said Frank.

Viv stopped laughing.

He looked at Frank.

He folded his arms and tapped a finger on his chin.

'That could work, you know. It has a nice ring to it.'

'Sounds dynamic.'

'It's got energy.'

'I like it', said Frank. 'It sounds like the future.'

Viv smiled.

'It is the future', he said.

By evening, Viv had taken over two of D.K.'s spare rooms.

One he was using as a bedroom.

The other, he and Frank had turned into a cross between an office and a cricketing headquarters.

It was from here that they would plan their next moves. And keep track of what Jago and his cronies were up to.

Dinner was served by D.K. in the kitchen.

Baked-bean curry, with naan.

He wasn't much of a cook.

They ate together, talking freely about everything that had happened over the past week. And what plans they had for the future.

For dessert, they shared half a tub of leftover ice cream, strawberry flavour, that D.K. had opened some time ago and forgotten about.

After that, D.K. made everyone a cup of peppermint tea.

'It has been quite a start to our enterprise, Mr Meadows, wouldn't you agree?'

Mr Chatterjee was standing beside the kitchen table.

'I never dreamed anything like this would happen to me', said Frank.

'It's incredible. Maybe a little scary, too. Jago is a dangerous man. And I don't like that Dorian much either.'

'But I'm glad we're doing it, Mr Chatterjee. I'm glad we're fighting back against The League, and everything they stand for.'

'Me too', said Viv, before taking a big gulp of tea.

He made a face.

'Ugh!' he exclaimed. 'That is disgusting.'

D.K. laughed.

'Have you never had a cup of peppermint tea, nephew?'

'No, I have not', said Viv, putting the cup down on the table before pushing it away.

'And I don't intend to have another one any time soon.'

'I don't mind it', said Frank.

'Well, you can have mine if you want', said Viv. 'I'm having an orange juice.'

'Help yourself', said D.K. 'You'll find some in the fridge.'

He pointed towards the far end of the kitchen.

'When you're ready, gentlemen, I'd like you to join me in my study. Now that we have eaten, and the excitements of the day have been put to bed, there are some things I must share with you. Important things.'

'Things that will take us further in our battle against The League.'

D.K. left the kitchen, cupping his peppermint tea in his hands.

Frank looked at Viv. They both felt a little of the excitement drain out of them, replaced not by fear, but by unease.

Mr Chatterjee's study was a large room with floor-to-ceiling windows. The view was of The Ancient Assembly of Cricket.

Neither Viv nor Frank had been in there before.

The walls were covered with framed photographs. Most of them contained Mr Chatterjee. Many of them also contained famous cricketers from around the world. And a select few contained his extended family, including, in a couple, Viv, his sister, and their parents.

D.K. sat behind the biggest desk Frank had ever seen.

It was made of oak. And it was vast.

On one corner there was a computer, a keyboard, and a mouse.

But mostly it was covered in documents.

Pieces of paper. Contracts. Print-outs. Newspapers.

Mr Chatterjee called to Frank and Viv as they entered.

'Come over here, gentlemen.'

He waved them round to his side of the desk.

As they approached, he cleared a space, sweeping documents to the left and right.

He reached into his pocket and produced a key, which he used to unlock a drawer set into the middle of the desk.

Frank watched as D.K. slipped his hand inside.

A moment passed as he felt around for something.

There was a short click, like a button being pressed. Followed by a second, longer click as a section of the desk-top popped open.

Viv and Frank blinked.

Both had seen the empty space cleared by D.K.

But neither had seen anything to suggest that a secret compartment was hidden beneath.

Mr Chatterjee reached across and extracted two thin, light-brown folders from their hiding place.

He held them up, then paused briefly.

The folders hovered in mid-air, caught between his thumb and his index finger.

It was like he was making a final decision. Confirming in his mind that he was doing the right thing.

'There's no turning back now, gentlemen. I hope you understand that. What you've done so far has been beyond the call of duty. Especially you, Frank.'

'If you want to quit, I will understand. It would be fine. Absolutely fine. Just say the word. But if you decide to stay. If you decide to carry on, you must realise that we cannot predict how The League of the Stuffed Shirts will react.'

'We cannot know what the mind of Jago Lilywhite Grace will choose to do.'

Silence filled the room.

It felt darker, colder, quieter than it had all evening.

D.K. knew he was asking a lot. He knew he was too old to do everything himself. He knew he needed Frank and Viv to help him.

Viv tipped his head to one side.

'We're in, Uncle. That right, Frank?'

Frank thrust out a hand and took the two files from Mr Chatterjee.

'Oh yes', he said. 'We're in all right. The League of the Stuffed Shirts isn't going to know what hit it.'

D.K. nodded.

'You are two outstanding young cricketers. And two outstanding young men. I couldn't ask for anyone better.'

'Jago brings out the worst in many people. But he has brought out the best in both of you.'

D.K. smiled, pushed back his chair, and stood up.

'Now, we have much to discuss. And it all begins with those.'

Feeling more alive than he had done in years, the old man, owner of the world's greatest bat company, leaned across and tapped the folders Frank was holding.

Frank and Viv looked at the front of the files.

They read the titles, each written in Mr Chatterjee's unmistakable handwriting.

And they knew, as they read them, that the next part of their adventure would take them a long way from London.

A long way from Accrington.

A long way from the safety and the comfort of what they knew.

The Artist, West Bengal, Right-Hand Bat was written on the first file in D.K.'s sloping script.

On the second folder, there was a more sinister legend.

Frank swallowed hard as he read it.

And a thousand questions started to form in his mind.

There was a trio of words, pressed close together, with a dash between them.

To many people, they would have been meaningless.

But not to Mr Chatterjee.

And not to Frank and Viv.

Written there, in black ink, was a set of words none of them wanted to see. A set of words that gave more questions than answers. A set of words that would change their understanding of The League of the Stuffed Shirts forever.

For the file read:

Number Two – Brother.

To be continued in …

The Unearthing of The Artist

The second book in the Fury Cricket XI

EXTRAS

FC

TO BAT, TO BOWL, TO DO

The Greatest Players

Every cricket innings has extras.

Wides, no balls, byes and leg byes.*

And Fury Cricket gives you extras as well!

In each book, we'll introduce you to a different squad of famous cricketers.

These are some of the greatest players to ever play the game.

Liam Taylor, esteemed journalist, has written pen portraits of these wonderful batters, bowlers, wicketkeepers and all-rounders.

And Neil Slater has produced fabulous caricatures of a select group of players.

So now the main event is over, sit back and enjoy the extras.

Let me introduce you to our first squad …

---

* A wide is when a bowler bowls the ball too far away for the batter to hit. A no ball is when the bowler bowls a high ball that doesn't bounce (which is dangerous), when they overstep the crease (thus gaining an unfair advantage), or when they bowl without a straight arm (also seen as gaining an advantage, because the bowler is throwing the ball instead of bowling it). A bye is when the batter doesn't hit the ball but manages to take a run anyway. And a leg bye is when the ball hits the batter's legs (or pads), and they take a run. Extras can add a lot to a total. The most extras ever conceded in a test match is 76! India were bowling against Pakistan at Bengaluru in December, 2007. They conceded 35 byes, 26 leg byes and 15 no balls. The only extra they managed to avoid was wides. In Pakistan's total of 537 all out, extras was the third-highest score, after Misbah-ul-Haq's 133 and Younis Khan's knock of 80.

THE ENTERTAINERS

Sometimes cricket can seem very serious, especially when you are desperate for your team to win.

But never forget that it is just a game, and games are about having fun!

Here is a squad of players who show the joy that the game can bring.

From exciting fast bowlers to fast-scoring batters, they truly deserve to be called The Entertainers.

With their attacking flair and dramatic style, they are the players that everyone is desperate to see.

Rohit Sharma, batter, India 2007-

They call him the Hitman, and with good reason. Nobody else has hit as many sixes in international cricket as Rohit Sharma, who has cleared the rope as many times as MS Dhoni and Yuvraj Singh combined.

With that kind of attacking flair, it is perhaps no surprise that he is the only player to score three double-centuries in one-day internationals, including 264 against Sri Lanka in 2014, the highest score of all time.

Sharma did not have an easy start in life: his parents were so poor that he had to go and live with his grandparents and uncles.

His cricketing abilities won him a scholarship to a school with better practice facilities.

But by his early twenties he was already one of the most expensive players in the IPL auctions, going on to captain the Mumbai Indians to five IPL titles.

In 152 international T20 matches, he has smashed an incredible 193 sixes.[*]

That's more than anybody else.

And in 2022 he was appointed captain of India's test side.

It just shows you that when you have drive, determination and the desire to develop your skills, you can achieve anything.

Rohit truly is a superstar.

And an Entertainer.

---

[*] All statistics in this section are correct at the time of writing. By the time you read this, Rohit may well have smashed even more sixes!

Brian Lara, batter, West Indies 1990-2007

In the 1990s the most exciting sight in cricket was watching Brian Lara bat.

He would crouch slightly in his stance and lift his bat so high it seemed to be touching the clouds.

And then his blade would flash down like lightning. He had an electric cover drive and a scintillating pull shot, which he sometimes played with his front leg lifted in the air.

Few batters in history have produced so many great innings.

Most spectacular were the world records.

In 1994 he hit 375 against England at St John's ground in Antigua, the highest ever test score at the time.

When his record was broken, he returned ten years later to the same ground, against the same opposition – and reclaimed the record with 400 not out.

And then there was his first-class record, a mind-boggling 501 not out for Warwickshire against Durham in 1994.

But perhaps his finest innings of all was 153 not out against Australia in 1999, steering his side to victory by one wicket as his batting partners fell around him.

By then the great West Indies were a fading force, but Lara single-handedly conjured up memories of their glory days.

Jos Buttler, batter, England 2011-

No England cricket fan will ever forget the moment when Jos Buttler collected a throw from Jason Roy and clipped off the bails – running out New Zealand's Martin Guptill and winning the 2019 World Cup for England off the final ball.

And it was Buttler's nerveless 59, in partnership with Ben Stokes, that gave England a chance in the first place.

Buttler might be England's greatest ever one-day batter.

His range of strokes and rapid scoring make him a nightmare for any bowling attack.

He plays many shots with a snap of the wrist that adds power and allows him to find the gaps, making it very difficult for opposing captains to set their field.

His calm personality also makes him a natural choice as captain for England's one-day sides, and he led them to victory in the 2022 T20 World Cup.

Buttler has lit up the IPL year after year with his explosive batting. He has eight T20 centuries in total, putting him joint fourth on the all-time list.

Viv Richards, batter, West Indies 1974-1991

Most players are nervous before it is their turn to bat. Not Viv Richards – he would just go to sleep.

His teammates woke him up when he was due in, then he would swagger out to the wicket in his cap, chewing gum.

Opponents were terrified of him.

The 'Master Blaster' hit the ball so hard that bowlers feared for their safety.

Richards was the most famous player in a West Indies team that was packed with stars.

In the summer of 1976, he scored 829 runs in just four tests against England.

A decade later he scored a test century in only 56 balls, setting a record that stood for thirty years.

Once Richards was playing in a match for Somerset when he missed a few balls in a row.

The bowler made a joke that Richards didn't know what the ball looked like, telling him that 'it's red, round and it's about five ounces'.

Richards hit the next ball for six into the river and said to the bowler: "You know what it looks like, now go and find it."

Barry Richards, batter, South Africa 1970-1970

Barry Richards was one of the most elegant, attacking batters of the 1970s. So why did he only play four tests for South Africa?

The answer, sadly, is politics. In those days South Africa had a racist government which would only let white people vote, even though most of the people in the country were black.

They would not even pick black players for the national cricket team!

So in 1970 other countries decided they would stop playing against South Africa until the government changed its rules.

That meant that Richards, who was white, never got much of a chance in international cricket.

Who knows what he might have achieved if he had played more games?

In the four tests that he did play, against Australia, he hit two centuries and averaged 73.

Instead, he played most of his cricket at domestic level, including for Hampshire in the English County Championship, scoring more than 28,000 runs at an average of 55.

Gilbert Jessop, batter, England 1899-1912

We all know how to score a six, right? Just hit the ball over the boundary without bouncing!

But the rules were different when Gilbert Jessop was playing, more than a hundred years ago.

Back then the only way to score a six was to hit the ball all the way out of the ground itself.

That didn't hold Jessop back. In his most famous innings, against Australia at the Oval in 1902, he reached his century off just 76 balls – a record that still stands today.

England chased down 263 to win the match by one-wicket, after Jessop had come in with the score at 48 for 5.

He even hit one of his shots onto the balcony where the players were sitting, but he only got four runs for it because of the rules at the time!

Jessop was the most attacking batter of his day, and crowds flocked to the ground whenever he was batting.

They nicknamed him 'the Croucher', because of his low stance, but his shot making was explosive. It was like he was playing one-day cricket before it had even been invented.

Virat Kohli, batter, India 2008-

In the decade of the 2010s, Virat Kohli scored nearly 21,000 international runs across all three formats of the game.

Nobody else even came close.

After the retirement of Sachin Tendulkar, it was Kohli who became the number one superstar in Indian cricket, and he rose to the challenge with ease.

During the 2023 World Cup he hit his fiftieth century in one-day international cricket, overtaking Tendulkar and becoming the first player ever to reach the milestone.

Kohli can score runs quickly and stylishly, but it is his personality which wins him a place in our team of The Entertainers.

He is an intense cricketer, always involved in the action, and it is impossible to take your eyes off him – whether he is batting or just prowling around in the field.

This is definitely one player that you should never pick a fight with, as his opponents have learned the hard way!

Kohli was also India's greatest-ever captain, before standing down in 2022.

With his fiercely competitive style, he brought a harder edge to Indian cricket, turning a team of talented individuals into the strongest side in the world.

Shoaib Akhtar, fast bowler, Pakistan 1997-2011

Edmund Hillary and Tenzing Norgay were the first people to reach the top of Mount Everest. Neil Armstrong was the first person to stand on the moon.

And in 2002 Shoaib Akhtar became the first person ever to bowl a cricket ball at 100 miles per hour.

Nobody has been recorded bowling faster than Shoaib.

If you try to imagine a fast bowler, you will probably imagine someone like Shoaib.

He sprinted in from a long run-up, eyes bulging, shirt rippling, hair flapping in the wind.

The media nicknamed him 'the Rawalpindi Express', after a high-speed train in Pakistan – but he actually bowled twice as fast as the train moves!

Shoaib was often injured, and sometimes he got into trouble for his attitude, which meant that he missed a lot of tests.

He did not take as many wickets as some other Pakistani bowlers, like Wasim Akram or Waqar Younis.

But when he was in form he was thrilling to watch.

In Kolkata in 1999 he clean bowled the great Indian batter Rahul Dravid with a yorker – and then did the same thing to Sachin Tendulkar next ball!

Brett Lee, fast bowler, Australia 2000-2012

During the early 2000s there was only one bowler who was as quick as Shoaib Akhtar: the blonde Australian paceman Brett Lee.

The two bowlers had different styles.

Shoaib used to hurl the ball down, getting power from his shoulder.

Lee had a much smoother action, coiling up in the delivery stride and then exploding through the crease.

Lee regularly bowled above 90 miles per hour and could reach 100 miles per hour on a good day.

At those speeds the batter has less than half a second to see the ball, judge its direction, and react.

Find a digital watch and try to time half a second.

Now imagine having to play a shot in that time!

Although Lee was very fast, he sometimes struggled to find the right line and length for his deliveries, which made them easier for batters to play.

You might want to compare his statistics to Glenn McGrath, another bowler who played for Australia at the same time.

Lee was faster, but McGrath more accurate.

Who do you think ended up taking more wickets?

But who was more entertaining to watch?

Ravindra Jadeja, All-rounder, India 2009-

Have your friends ever made jokes about you? It's not nice, is it?

When Ravindra Jadeja started his cricket career, people on the internet used to make horrible jokes about him too. But he didn't listen to them. He knew he was a good cricketer – and he has been proving it ever since.

His greatest strength is his left-arm spin bowling, which is very difficult for batters to play against, especially on India's turning wickets.

But he is also a skilled batter – so good, in fact, that he scored three triple centuries in first-class cricket by the time he was 23.

And then there is his brilliant catching and throwing. Many people consider him to be the best fielder in the world.

Possibly the greatest of all time.

Jadeja is a fantastic entertainer too, which is why we have included him in this squad.

Look at his celebration when he scores a century – he twirls his bat around at high speed, as though it is a sword!

So next time somebody makes a joke about you, just remember the story of Ravindra Jadeja, the man who made the bullies look stupid.

Shane Warne, leg-spinner, Australia 1992-2007

The place was Old Trafford, Manchester.

The date was 4th June 1993.

The batter was Mike Gatting.

A young Australian spinner called Shane Warne stepped up to bowl his first delivery in test cricket in England, his blonde hair shining in the sun.

The ball dipped in the air, pitching a long way outside leg stump.

And then it span – all the way past Gatting, past his bat, and into the top of his off stump.

It was so good that people called it "the ball of the century".

There has never been another cricketer like Warne. He had his leg-breaks, his top-spinner, his googly, his flipper – but his greatest weapon was his brain.

He was forever thinking about new ways to fool batters, and he often made them look very foolish indeed.

And he was always the most confident player on the pitch, never doubting that he could get the batters out.

During Warne's career Australia became the best side in the world, winning World Cups and Ashes series many times.

His favourite matches were against England. He took 195 wickets against them in tests, a big chunk of his overall tally of 708.

'We only wish you were English!' sang the England fans when he played against them for the final time. And wasn't that the truth?

Shaheen Shah Afridi, fast bowler, Pakistan 2018-

Take a tennis ball. Wrap it in sticky tape. You now have a 'tape ball'. This is what most people use to play cricket in Pakistan, where there are special tape ball leagues.

The ball moves even faster through the air than a real cricket ball, so it is a good way to develop your skills.

One player who learnt cricket by playing tape ball was Shaheen Shah Afridi.

It was only in 2015, when he was 15 years old, that he first played with a hard ball.

Three years later he was making his debut for Pakistan, and a year later he became the youngest bowler ever to take a five-wicket haul in a World Cup match.

Afridi uses his tall height and lightning pace to get batters out. And he is especially dangerous with the new ball.

He also has a brilliant 'yorker' – a delivery aimed at the batter's toes so that the ball squeezes under the bat.

He says he learned to bowl it in his youth while playing tape ball. 'Every Pakistan bowler loves bowling yorkers,' he once said. But we're not sure every opposing batter likes to face them!

Ian Botham, all-rounder, England 1976-1992

It was the summer of 1981, England were playing Australia, and Ian Botham was the English captain.

His side lost the first test.

In the second, which was drawn, he didn't score a single run.

Then he got sacked from the captaincy.

Things weren't going well.

The third test, at Headingley, seemed to be going even worse for England and they were heading for an innings defeat.

Then out walked Botham to bat.

He hit 149 not out, smashing the ball all over the ground, and England won the game.

They won the next one too, after Botham took five wickets for just one run.

And the next one, after Botham hit 118 in just 102 balls.

It was like a fairy tale, not real life.

Botham – or 'Beefy', as his teammates called him – was a six-hitting batter, a brilliant slip fielder, and an outstanding swing bowler.

And he liked to party too!

In the 1980s he was probably the most famous sportsperson in England, from any sport.

Fans loved him because of the way he played the game: always attacking, always entertaining, never giving up.

Kapil Dev, all-rounder, India 1978-1994

When a team is more than 200 runs behind in the first innings of a test match, their opponents can make them bat again right way (or 'follow on').

That looked like it was going to happen to India in a test match against England in 1990.

With only one wicket left, they still needed 24 runs to avoid the follow-on.

But Kapil Dev had other ideas: he hit four sixes in a row, back over the bowler's head, to get the runs required.

That was just how Kapil played. In the 1983 World Cup his team were struggling in a match against Zimbabwe.

He walked out and hit 175 off just 138 balls. In the end India won the tournament, their first ever World Cup, and Kapil was the captain. It was such a famous victory that it has even been turned into a movie.

And we haven't even mentioned his bowling yet! He was an excellent fast bowler, at a time when most other good Indian bowlers were spinners. At the time he retired he held the record for the most wickets in test cricket. He was a true all-rounder and a natural entertainer.

Brendon McCullum, wicketkeeper, New Zealand 2002-2016

As a player, Brendon McCullum was good at starting things.

In the first ever match in the IPL, in 2008, he blasted 158 not out for the Kolkata Knight Riders, hitting 13 sixes from the 73 deliveries he faced.

And he was good at ending things too.

In his last ever test match, in 2016, he hit the fastest ever test hundred, reaching his century off just 54 balls.

Those two innings show what a spectacular player he could be.

But his greatest impact was as a leader. The New Zealand team improved quickly under his captaincy, and the players around him were inspired by his attacking, entertaining approach to the game.

More recently, he has been working as the coach of the England cricket team, but his ideas haven't changed.

Together with Ben Stokes, the England captain, he has encouraged players to go out and play with freedom.

England have scored at a very fast rate, pulling off some amazing victories along the way.

McCullum's nickname is 'Baz', so the media say that England are playing a new style of cricket called 'Bazball'.

He doesn't like the name, but it has stuck.

Maybe because it makes everyone who hears it think of one thing: explosive, entertaining, exciting cricket.

Discover More About The Entertainers

You can find statistics for all the players at www.espncricinfo.com.

There you can discover how many runs they scored, how many wickets they took, and how many catches they held.

And if you want to see The Entertainers in action, why not head to YouTube to find videos of them playing sensational shots, bowling unplayable balls, and holding unbelievable catches.

Acknowledgements

The Fury Cricket Team have been hard at work throughout the development of the book.

I'd like to say a huge thank you to all of them for their skill, determination and effort in helping get it ready for you, the reader!

So, in no particular order, thanks to:

Penny, for her fantastic editing.

Sophie, for her design master skills.

Conor, for his fabulous font-making and legendary logos.

Rory, for his brilliant illustrations.

David, for his ideas, energy, and enthusiasm.

Dawn, for her insights and support.

Liam, for his research, writing and encyclopaedia of cricketing knowledge.

Neil, for his classic caricatures.

About the Author

The idea for Fury Cricket first came to Mike when he was watching the Indian Premier League.

Despite having written forty books for adults (mostly about teaching), Mike dreamed of writing stories since he was a little boy.

So, one day, he decided to sit down and do something about it.

Fury Cricket was born.

The Search for The Stump Smasher is the first book in the series.

Mike had so much fun writing it, he nearly fell off his chair laughing (well, he would have done, if his chair didn't have arm rests).

He hopes you have even more fun reading it and becoming part of the Fury Cricket Club.

The world needs great stories, just like it needs great cricketers. Brave, determined, and ready to take on adventures.

Cricketers just like you.

Enjoy the book … and see you for the next one!

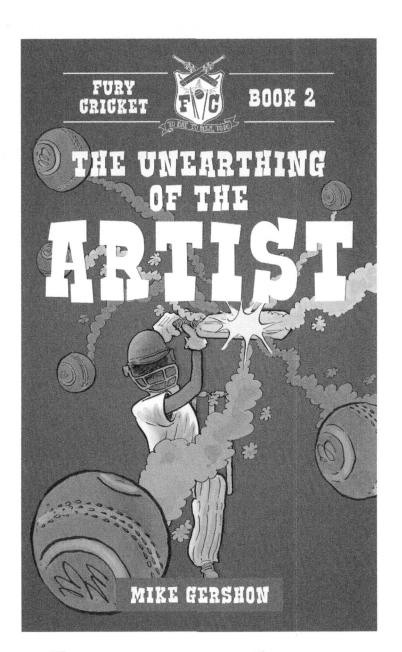

Find it now on Amazon

Find it now on Amazon

Printed in Great Britain
by Amazon

45490745R00131